John Thomas Haines

My Poll and my partner Joe; a nautical drama, in three acts

The music selected and arranged by Mr. Jolly

John Thomas Haines

My Poll and my partner Joe; a nautical drama, in three acts
The music selected and arranged by Mr. Jolly

ISBN/EAN: 9783337305642

Printed in Europe, USA, Canada, Australia, Japan

Cover: Foto ©Andreas Hilbeck / pixelio.de

More available books at **www.hansebooks.com**

"MY POLL AND MY PARTNER JOE."

A NAUTICAL DRAMA,

In Three Acts,

BY JOHN THOMAS HAINES, ESQ.

The Music selected and arranged by Mr. Jolly.

PRINTED FROM THE ACTING COPY, WITH REMARKS,
BIOGRAPHICAL AND CRITICAL, BY D.—G.

To which are added,

A DESCRIPTION OF THE COSTUME,—CAST OF THE CHARACTERS,—
ENTRANCES AND EXITS,—RELATIVE POSITIONS OF THE
PERFORMERS ON THE STAGE,—AND THE WHOLE OF
THE STAGE BUSINESS,

As performed at the

ROYAL SURREY THEATRE.

EMBELLISHED WITH A FINE ENGRAVING,

By Mr. BONNER, from a Drawing taken in the Theatre, by
Mr. R. CRUIKSHANK.

LONDON:

JOHN CUMBERLAND, 2, CUMBERLAND TERRACE,
CAMDEN NEW TOWN.

REMARKS.

"My Poll and my Partner Joe."

NATIONALITY becomes a virtue when it springs from feelings inspired by the land of our birth. "The man that don't like *England*," exclaimed honest Jack Fuller, in the heat of parliamentary debate, "*damn him, let him leave it !*"

In turning over the page of history, we contemplate with enthusiasm the martial prowess of our ancestors, who were called to defend not only their own liberties, but those of mankind. Britain has maintained her proud supremacy among nations through a long series of ages; trampled down stern oppression, that threatened, and (with her own glorious exception) had well nigh spread abroad, universal anarchy; and crowned the august work by giving peace to the world, and freedom to the slave.

Whatever brings to our recollection the triumphs of the past deserves our gratitude; but when genius applies itself to the task, how truly it commands our admiration! The deeds of heroes were the favourite theme of the poets of old, and their noblest strains were devoted to immortalise patriotism and valour.

Blessings on the memory of the bard, " and palms eternal flourish round his urn," who first struck his lyre to celebrate the wooden walls, and the brave, generous, Jack Tars of unconquered and unconquerable Old England! If earth hide him, light be the green turf on his breast; if ocean cover him, calm be the wave on its surface !— May his spirit find rest where souls are blessed, and his body be shrined in the holiest cave of the deep and silent sea !

Among the naval lyrics that roused and kept alive the ardent spirit of our seamen is "My Poll and my Partner Joe." We remember when every manly heart beat to this national melody; but other tastes ("the fruits of calm times and a long peace") are come upon us; we have little sympathy for past glories. "Ye Mariners of England," and "Here, a sheer Hulk, lies poor Tom Bowling," are lost in ("Most Forcible Feeble!") "Oh, no, we never mention her," and "I'd be a Butterfly."

"My Poll and my Partner Joe," once so sweetly vocal, is now instrumental in filling many bright eyes with tears, and the manager's purse with money. This English song has suggested to Mr. Haines a drama as truly English, and that promises to rival it in popularity.

In Harry Hallyard we behold a British tar, bold as Mars, brawny as Hercules, and comely as Adonis; in Joe Tiller, his friend and partner in a trim-built wherry, a lad with a soul equally fiery, but a body of less herculean dimensions. If Harry's *prose* is of greater unction, Joe's *verse* is more than a match for it; for Joe builds the lofty rhyme where the sea-mew does its nest, mounted aloft on the top-mast head. Among the sailor's many virtues, prudence and worldly wisdom are not generally the most shining; yet Hal is an exception; for, though deeply enamoured of his pretty Poll, he resolves not to marry until industry has put him in possession of some ready hand.   An unexpected appeal to his generosity introduces two very opposite characters — Black Brandon, the captain of a slave-ship, and Sam, a supreme oddity, a bailiff's tail, timid, snuffling, and quaintly pragmatical; with one eye blocked up, and the other set in garnets! Hal's savings are applied to rescue an ancient, broken-down mess-mate from the rude grasp of this raggamuffin body-snatcher, and the wedding is about to be postponed, when Mary Maybud, commonly called "Pretty Poll of Putney," charmed with the generous self-denial of her sailor, proffers him her hand, which is accepted with prompt enthusiasm; and Watchful Waxend, a psalm-singing cobler and the Bishop of Battersea, is deputed forthwith to solemnise the holy rites; a task of no small difficulty to that devout prelate, seeing that his red nosed reverence is ever on the reel with a crozier in one hand, and an ale-jug in the other.   The jolly young watermen and their lasses are assembled, the fiddles are going, and the punch is getting pretty freely on board, when an ugly customer intrudes, escorting a press-gang, who exercise without delay their detestable trade.   Joe claims protection as waterman to a fire-office, but for Harry there is no retreating: the Phœnix cannot restore him to his lady-bird, nor the Norwich Union accelerate his own.   For this good office he is indebted to his gruff friend; but 'tis useless to kick against the pricks, and every black bristle in the beard of sable Brandon rises in retribution for an insult that Hal's just indignation had offered to this savage trafficker in human flesh.   The parting between the distracted lovers; Harry's consignment of his pretty Poll to the brotherly guardianship of his partner Joe; his adventures on board the Polyphemus; the capture of a slave-ship; the liberation of the negroes; the ludicrous recognition of the Battersea Bishop in the odour of sanctity, who saves Hal's life by a well-directed shot from a beer-barrel; the storming and blowing-up of the strong-hold of the slavers; negro gratitude; "tremendous explosion;" and a fearful catalogue of etceteras that occupy an interval of four years, are best described by the scenery, machinery, and performers of the "Royal Surry."— The sequel is mournful: Harry returns rich in fame and fortune, accompanied by the soaking prelate, who, in manners, costume, attitude, and physiognomy, is so whimsically metamorphised into a sea-monster, as to leave but few traces of his former identity.   Hal, in his long absence, had been killed by the newspapers; and Mary, following the example of Southerne's heroine, Isabella, marries Joe Tiller, and greets her first love on his return with the astounding intelligence.— The surprise, sorrow, and indignation of Harry Hallyard; the remorse, shame, and agony of the despairing wife, were finely depicted by T. P. Cooke and Miss Macarthy.   The accidental death of Partner Joe at this sad crisis terminates the tragic scene; he dies as he lived with honour; but *Honner* (too good an actor to be thus prematurely cut off) dies not with him.

It is pleasant to behold an audience crammed to the roof expressing their sympathy with the scene by silence and tears, and shouting their emulation of fun and drollery with uproarious delight;—it is pleasant to behold our happy countrymen, with their sweethearts and wives, leaving the pandemoniums of treason to their buffoon mendicants, and enjoying a few hours of rational entertainment.   Who cares for *Tom Duncombe*, when he can see (a much better actor!) *Tom Cooke?*—Or Partner *Joe*, (*of Middlesex!*) when he can make merry with the *Bishop of Battersea?*   The Church in danger!   By the rubicund proboscis of the right reverend Hierach! we would pull the caitiff by the nose (as the devil's chaplain did Carlisle, and Saint Dunstan did the devil!) who should raise such a false alarm!   The Bishop in his pulpit was hailed by a full pit, and in *both* sees was equally popular !—a cobler-prelate in leather-pontificalibus ; a black-muzzled Jack Tar in blue jacket and trousers, with a portentous pig-tail, from which depended a holyday rosette of true blue ! Talk of cheap knowledge and penny politics ! Here a man may be happy for six hours for sixpence ; aye, and (liberty and equality for ever !) *look down* upon his master !

We are not in love with sentimentality (like virtue !) for itself alone. No man likes mustard *per se.* In this drama our sympathies are awakened by justice and humanity, and 'tis highly seasoned with a plentiful infusion of fun. By virtue of the latter commodity, we are reconciled to Mr. Sam Snatchem, and swallow with epicurean greediness his rich morsels of equivoque and pun. His delicate appreciation of Poll's pretty foot (" 'Tis not like a *pickaxe*—as much *behind* as *before !*") redeemed his queer obliquity of vision, and unique breeches and top-boots. This prime buffoon, in the person of Mr. Asbury, was *sui generis.*—The law of arrest loses its terrors in such a scarecrow representative : were Sam to pop in his head among his old acquaintances in the house when the motion is discussed, the bill would be lost !

Great praise is due to Mr. T. P. Cooke, Miss Macarthy, and our pious friend the bishop, Mr. W. Smith. We were much amused with the nimble-tongued loquacity of (Miss Martin) a west-end milliner, and cher ami of the prelate's ! The house rang with her orthographical *variations*, that would have puzzled *Wulker*, given old *Tom Sheridan* a fit of the cholic, and contributed some new readings to the excellent work now in progress of the venerable *father* of Sheridan Knowles.

Mr. Haines has chosen a happy subject, and treated it happily ; and Mr. Davidge, by its adoption, deserves the unprecedented success that has attended its production. Let the public be won by patriotic spectacles, and we shall not have cause to lament that our national character among the humbler orders of society is degenerated into apathetic, not to say brutal, indifference. Though *now* dwelling in peace, the trumpet of war may ere long startle us from our pleasant dream of security ; and to whom shall we *then* look for protection ? Not the mischievous brawlers in high life and low—for base poltroons they are, and timid as treacherous—but the brave spirits who have done us good service in the hour of peril, and whose glorious example has inspired a succession of youthful heroes to conquer or die for their country ! It is wise to infuse the *amor patriæ* into popular amusements : national songs work wonders among the million. In Little Russia, no sooner are postillions mounted for a journey, than they begin to hum a patriotic air, which they often continue for hours without intermission. The soldiers sing during a long and fatiguing march ; the peasant lightens his labour in the same manner ; and in a still evening, the air vibrates with the cheerful songs of surrounding villages.

Peace to the souls of the heroes whose bones lie mouldering in the battle-field ! On England's glory—now nerveless, cold, and (thanks to the barking, foul-mouthed curs of democracy !) almost dead,— on England's glory shall the brave, long-tried patriot inscribe " RE-SURGAM !"—for WELLINGTON has not conquered nor NELSON died in vain !

D.——G.

Cast of the Characters,

As performed at the Surrey Theatre, September 7, 1835.

Captain Oakheart } of H. M. Sloop Polyphemus	{ Mr. Bannister.
Lieutenant Manly }	{ Mr. Tully.
Black Brandon (Captain of a Slaver) . .	Mr. Dillon.
Ben Bowse (Boatswain of ditto) . . .	Mr. Cullen.
Zinga (a Negro)	Mr. C. Pitt.
Harry Hallyard (the Pride of Battersea Hard)	Mr. T. P. Cooke.
Joe Tiller (his Friend and Partner) . .	Mr. R. Honner.
Watchful Waxend (a Psalm-Singing Cobler, }	} Mr. W. Smith.
nicknamed the " Bishop of Battersea") . }	
Will Wall-it (of the Crown and Crozier) .	Mr. Young.
Sam Snatchem (a Bailiff) . . .	Mr. Asbury.
Old Sam Sculler (a Waterman) . .	Mr. Mortimer.
Sentinel of the Slaver	Mr. Debar.
Mary Maybud (called " Pretty Poll of Putney")	Miss Macarthy.
Abigail Holdforth (from Bullock-Smithey) . .	Miss Martin.
Zamba (a Negress)	Miss Cross.
Dame Hallyard	Mrs. Stickney.

Sailors, Soldiers, Piccarooners, Slaves, Watermen, Lasses, &c.

Costume.

CAPT. OAKHEART and **LIEUT. MANLY.**—Naval uniforms.

BLACK BRANDON.—*First dress:* Long pea coat—red waistcoat—rough blue cloth trousers—glazed hat—shoes and buckles. *Second dress:* Blue jacket—petticoat trousers—check shirt—leather belt and buckle.

HARRY HALLYARD.—*First dress:* Waterman's scarlet jacket, &c. *Second dress:* Sailor's nankeen suit. *Third dress:* Sailor's blue suit.

JOE TILLER.—*First dress:* Blue brummagem, with a fireman's badge — blue breeches — white hose — shoes and buckles. *Second dress:* Brummagem—white jacket—low-crowned hat, with crape-band.

OLD SAM SCULLER.—Old green brummagem—red waistcoat—plush trousers—shoes and buckles—low-crowned hat.

WATCHFUL WAXEND. — *First dress:* Red waistcoat, with sleeves—black breeches, with red and black patches on the seat—red hose and nightcap—shoes and buckles. *Second dress:* Brown coat glazed hat—black neckerchief—leather apron, &c. *Third dress:* Sailor's jacket, bound with canvass—very large blue trousers—check shirt—tremendous whiskers—long pig-tail, with blue ribbon at the end—high straw hat, with blue ribbons.

WILL WALL-IT.—Waterman's old suit.

SAM SNATCHEM.—Shabby green coat—queer top-boots—white hat.

BEN BOWES.—Sailor's blue suit.

ZINGA.—White trunks and shirt—black arms and leggings—black belt and buckle.

MARY MAYBUD.—*First dress:* Old-fashioned light chintz gown, with the tail drawn up—red skirt—straw hat and ribbons—muslin apron, &c. *Second dress:* Half-mourning cotton gown—white neckerchief—black mittens.

ABIGAIL HOLDFAST.—*First dress:* Chintz gown, drawn up—scarlet skirt—straw hat, &c. *Second dress:* Handsome yellow sarsnet pelisse—crimson sarsnet gown—straw bonnet, with large white veil, and ostrich feathers.

DAME HALLYARD. — Old-fashioned dark chintz gown—black mittens—mob cap—white apron.

ZAMBA.—White frock—mob cap—red shoes.

"MY POLL AND MY PARTNER JOE."

ACT I.

SCENE I.—*Interior of the Crown and Crozier Public House at Battersea—the Hard, or Landing-Place, seen at the back, and the opposite shore visible through the large window—boats passing and re-passing as the curtain ascends.*

WATERMEN *discovered seated, smoking and drinking—*OLD SAM SCULLER *reading a newspaper—*WATCHFUL WAXEND *seated near him, tipsy—*WILL WALL-IT, *the Landlord, attending—the company laughing.*

Wax. (C.) You may laugh, you profane scoffers ; but I stick like wax to my religious spirit.

Wal. (R.) That you do, Master Waxend, and to my full-proof spirit, too !   [*They all laugh.*

Wax. You're all going by steam to the diabolical oven —drinking and sotting from morning till night ! [*To Wall-it.*] Fill my pot ! You'll be thirsty enough in the next world, and no beer : there they allows none to be drunk on the premises.

Wal. [*Bringing beer.*] Your beer, Master Watchful.— Money :

Wax. Oh, stick it up. [*Turning to the Watermen.*] Don't trust me, but read the Psalms of Thomas Paine, and the commen—com-en-tatories of Julius Cæsar.

        [*They all laugh.*

Enter JOE TILLER *from the Hard,* L. C.

Joe. Harry Halliyard not here yet !

Then I must forth again to wander by the river,
To see if I my par-tener, and kind friend can diskiver.

Wax. Ah, Master Joe, you're a poet : why don't you turn your thoughts to holy subjects ?—Why don't you do as somebody did—write a legacy in a country churchyard ?

Joe. An elegy, you mean.

Wax. Well, I know; some people call 'em 'tother way. [*Drinking.*] All the world's a sot! [*Drinking again.*] Ah, you little think how drinking wears out the soul!

Joe. So much the better for you cobblers.

> If drinking wears the soul away,
>   Why, add a little leather;
> For, till our welting does decay,
>   We'll drink and stick together.

All. Bravo! capital, Joe! hurra!

Wax. That would make a capital psalm. I'll uplift my voice. [*Singing loudly.*] "If drinking wears——"

Scu. [*Rising.*] Hold your tongue, Master Waxend.— I've got athwart of the account of the great battle of late; here's a full list of the killed.

All. [*Rising, and coming forward.*] Oh, let us hear— let us hear!

Wal. [*Crossing to Sculler.*] Is Dan Deadeye there?

Scu. No.

Wal. Or Sam Scupper? or Charley Coil? or Mick Marline.

Scu. No, no.

Wal. I'm glad of that—they left a long score unpaid. Now I shouldn't mind if Ben Binnacle was popped off; he was the only one as paid his shot afore he sailed; and I've got his shore togs in keeping.

Scu. [*Starting.*] What's this? Harry Heartly dead! Harry! Poor fellow! poor fellow!

Joe. (L.) What! Harry that you were bound for?— That's bad news, Master Sculler; he'll never come back to pay his debt.

Scu. (L. C.) No, Joe; and if they come upon the poor old waterman, why, they must e'en sell his boat, and make a beggar of him at once.

Joe. That'll be hard; let's hope better: no one would be Philistine enough to rob a poor white-headed old man of his last crust.

Wax. (R. C.) Philistine!—Ha! the Philistines were common robbers—all Dick Turpins, every one of them.

Joe. You're too learned for us, Master Watchful; but I will say, it's a hard law:

> For if a man is taken to prison,
>   And stripped of every thing that's his'n,
> 'Twere better far to stop his wizzen.

All. Capital! capital!

Wal. Bravo, Master Joe !—Why, you're quite the Byron of Battersea !

Joe. [*Modestly.*] I does a little poetical poetry ; it comes natural to me.

Wax. [*Standing on a chair, and drinking.*] Yes, the spirit naturally gets over us. Hear me preach.

All. [*Pushing him off the chair.*] No, no ! no preaching.

Joe. Come, don't be cast down, Master Sculler. Where's Harry Halliyard ? I've got a little present for him—something as I've been writing about his pretty Poll—his Poll. Well, he desarves her, for a better lad with a truer heart never feathered an oar.

Scu. Right, lad ; Harry's the pride of the Hard, and Mary's the prettiest, aye, and the most industrious wench on either side of the River. I'ts a pleasure to see her little fingers go—stitch, stitch, hem, hem, from morning till night. She's been a daughter to me, since her father died. Poor fellow, his was a brave end. Well, as I was saying, she's looked up to me because I was his friend ; and a neater Cabin than old Sam Sculler's a'n't to be found near the Thames—all her work. And now, if these harpies come for poor Heartly's debt, they'll sell up all the sticks, and leave the old man without a rag of canvas to weather out his days. [*Sighing.*] Well, well !

Joe. But they won't do that, Master Sculler ; come, come, keep a good heart. But, as I was telling you, I've written a something about Mary.

All. Let us hear.

Joe. [*Taking out a paper.*] Here it is. I——

Wax. Them charity schools is a good thing. [*All laugh.*

Joe. Ah, laugh away—they are a good thing. How many children they save from depravity ! how many do they teach the difference between a brute and a man ! I learnt in one ; and I should think I was unworthy the charity shown to me, if I ever stooped to deny it : for, mark ye, my lads,—

When the mountains so high are kiver'd with snows,
What a very cold wind from the top of 'em blows !
But when great ones and rich ones are kind all the while,
What a very warm sun's for the poor in their smile !

Scu. Good lad ! good lad !

Wax. [*Tipsy, singing loudly.*] "When them mountains so high "—common time—" when—"

All. [*Stopping him.*] Silence ! silence ! — Let's hear Joe's verses.

Joe. Now, lads. [*Reading.*]

> Near Putney Bridge there lived a maid,
> " More bright than May-day morn—"

Wax. Oh, stop! stop!—I've heard something like that in a hymn—long metre. [*Singing.*]

> " On Richmond Hill there lived a lass,
> More bright than May-day morn."

Watermen. Oh, fie! oh!

Joe. [*Offended.*] Well, I'll never write no more. I'm no pirate—I never steals another man's ideas; at all events, you can never be robbed. [*They all go up, and sit.*

Enter BLACK BRANDON, R. S. E.—*the Landlord bows to him—he advances sullenly, and takes a seat, eyeing the company.*

Bra. This is the Crown and Crozier?

Wal. It is, sir; the best house above bridge for comfort and respectable company.

Bra. [*Sneeringly.*] So I perceive. Bring me some rum: I have business in this neighbourhood.

Wal. Can I assist you in——

Bra. [*Surlily.*] You can—bring the rum, and be hanged to you!   [*Exit Wall-it, muttering,* R.

Wax. [*Drawing his seat near Brandon.*] Sir, were you ever among the Niggers?

Bra. [*Starting, and looking fiercely at him.*] Why do you ask?

Wax. You'd make a capital slave-driver.

Bra. Dare you insult me?

Wax. Don't wax wrath, or I shall bristle up myself.—Hear me preach!

Bra. Psha! fool!

> [*He thrusts Waxend back, who falls over his seat—the Watermen rise tumultuously.*

Joe. [*Interposing.*] Come, come, sir; you are forgetting yourself, and insulting the clergy. This is the Bishop of Battersea; and—

> If the church is knocked down with such gaiety,
> Why, there'll be pretty pickings for the laiety.

Bra. Am I among madmen here? Oh, here's the rum.

Re-enter WALL-IT, R.

Hark ye, landlord: is there one Sculler, a waterman, living in these parts?

Scu. [*Coming forward.*] My name's Sculler—Old Sam Sculler.

Bra. You had a friend named Heartly?

Scu. Ah, poor fellow!—I have just read of his death.

Bra. Then you must be aware he can't pay a certain debt he owed, and that you are bound for it—here's the agreement, and so, old gentleman, hand over the rhino.

Scu. Great Heaven! I'm a ruined man!

Bra. [*Drinking.*] This rum's not so bad.

Scu. You will give me time to look about me.

Bra. I want the money! [*Going to* R. S. E., *and beckoning off.*] You must talk to this gentleman about time.

Enter SAM SNATCHEM, R. S. E.—*he crosses to Sculler,* L.

Bra. [*Pointing to Sculler.*] There's your prisoner!

Wax. Oh, my lapstone! what a gentleman! Baalam and his ass! Oh, ye captivators of corpusses! hear my voice.

Bra. [*To Waxend.*] Silence! or I'll spoil your voice for a month to come. [*To Sculler.*] Where's the rhino?

Scu. (L. C.) If you insist on your demand, I am a beggar.

Bra. (C.) Away with him!

Sna. You see, my old cove, here's the parchment—no gammon about it—all reg'lar. So you'd better out with the yellow 'uns, and stash all patter.

Scu. I must sell my boat.

Sna. To be sure; you must put up the floater. Take my adwice; I'm the honest chap as is—has a feeling for the misfortunate: never resist the law; if a man claims your vestcoat, let him have it, or you'll lose your kicksies in trying the argument.

Bra. Away with him!

Joe. (R. C.) This is too bad. What, lads, will you see Old Sam Sculler, a man whose hairs are grown white in honesty and industry, dragged like a dog to a gaol? [*Crossing to Snatchem.*] Let go your hold!

Sna. Don't resist the law. Take my adwice: if a man kicks you, rub the place; for if you strike agin, ten to one if you has witnesses as to who was the degressor.

Watermen. Down with them! down with them!

Bra. Look to your prisoner. Stand back, I say!

[*He thrusts Sculler over to Snatchem, throws himself between them and the approaching Watermen, and levels a pistol at them.*]

Wax. [*Running behind, and jumping on a chair.*] I'm a man of peace—hear me preach!

Bra. Quick! quick! away!

[*Snatchem is dragging Sculler towards the door,* R. S. E.

Enter HARRY HALLIYARD, *suddenly,* L. S. E.—*he darts forward hastily, and knocks Snatchem's hat over his eyes, seizes Brandon's pistol, throws him round to the corner,* L., *and points it at him.*

Harry. Ahoy! what boats are foul here? An old wherry run down by a coal-barge! Damme! stand back!

[*A loud shout, and a momentary picture of consternation and surprise.*

Bra. Who the devil are you, that board strangers like a red squall, without leave or notice!

Harry. Who am I? I'm the happiest dog on the Thames; got the best craft, and the prettiest sweetheart; will pull a match with any man between bridges; know how to serve a friend, 'specially an old one; always pay my rent; can wash my own shirts; and hate lawyers.— Now who the devil are you?

Sna. [*Pushing up the hat from his eyes.*] Don't resist the law—take my adwice.

Harry. So I will, lad. [*Knocking his hat over his eyes again—the Watermen follow Harry's example, and hustle him from one to the other.*

Scu. (R. C.) [*Interposing.*] Don't, lads, don't! Hark ye, Harry; you are a fine fellow, and I know will listen to reason. This is Harry Heartly's debt; he, poor fellow! is dead, and——

Harry. (C.) Harry dead!—Poor Harry! Well, but who's this gentleman that's come to shoot us all?

Bra. (L.) I demand payment of the debt.

Wax. (L. C.) When the devil demands his due, then look out: you'll be saying you knew me, but I'll send notice that I never kept such company.

Bra. A truce to this foolery! Am I to be paid, or must the man go to prison?

Harry. Why, look ye, sir: if your demand be a just one, it would be folly to resist.

Sna. That's right—take my adwice!

Harry. It would be vain to resist, as I've said; but you would never be so stone-hearted as to strip an old man of the hard earnings of sixty years of weary toil, and that, too, for a debt not his own. To pay your demand, he must sell his boat; then what remains for him? He must go to the workhouse; the winter of his days must be passed at the fireless hearth of charity, after having honestly toiled away his summer to build himself a home of independence. You

wouldn't it break the old man's heart?—Or, if you would, your own must be of stone so hard, that all the paviors of London couldn't break it up to macadamize one foot of road to the poorhouse, the last resting place you would send him to.

Bra. (L. C.) All the preaching in the world won't talk me out of my debt: my money, or a prison for him.

All. Shame! shame!

Harry. Hold, friends! Here, I will be bail for him, and Will Wall-it, here, will be bound with me.

Wal. (R.) That I will!

Scu. (L.) Thank you, lads! thank you!

Harry. [*To Brandon.*] And, do you hear? do you and your devil's imp beat down to the old man's house in half an hour; and if my Poll is what I think her, we'll board you in the smoke of a salute you little expect. Lead the way, landlord. [*To Sculler.*] Cheerly, old heart!—'Tisn't every squall that captizes a boat.—Cheerly! cheerly!

All. Hurra! hurra!

[*Exeunt Harry, cheering,* R. S. E., *Sculler and the rest shouting—Snatchem is following, when Wax-end, who is sitting at the back,* R., *knocks his hat over his eyes, and the scene closes.*

SCENE II.—*A Room in Sculler's House.*

Enter MARY MAYBUD, *with needle-work, followed by* ABIGAIL HOLDFORTH, L.

Abi. (L. C.) And so, seeing you at work, you see, ma'am, I thought I'd make bold to ask you.

Mary. (C.) Well, but my good girl, London is a large place, and the industrious never need starve in it. What trade are you?

Abi. I'm a shoe-binder, ma'am, from Bullock Smithey. I'm a girl of moral perpensities, can sing a psalm, or beat a carpet; and, as for turning a corner in the binding-way, leave me alone for neatness.

Mary. But what made you come away from your own town?

Abi. There it is: one of my moral perpensities got the better of me—I fell in love.

Mary. And not being able to meet a return, you ran away from the object?

Abi. No, I run'd after the object: he was obliged to

emigrate through a misfortune—a wicked hussy swore a filiation to him.

Mary. Then you should endeavour to forget him.

Abi. I can't forget him; and I thought it was best to come away, for fear they should swear something of that sort to me.

Mary. I am sorry I cannot serve you; I am an orphan, and obliged to work for every meal. I am content to do so, because I think, some how, that the bread we have earned must eat the sweeter. I am a stranger, too, to London; I never travel farther from Putney than just down the river in Harry's boat to Westminster Bridge—yes, once I made a voyage to Hungerford Market. So, you see, my good girl, I could direct you but badly; but if you had written to this lover of yours——

Abi. I did, bless you!

Mary. Then you know his direction?

Abi. Oh, yes: the girl at the huckster's shop wrote three times for me, and I saw the letters carefully directed, "Mr. Watchful Waxend, London."

Mary. [*Aside.*] So, so, Mr. Watchful! [*Aloud.*] You had better look in again towards evening; I have an old friend here who can, perhaps, advise you.

Abi. I'm much obliged to me. Be so good as to say that I can turn my hand to anything: I can hem and seam, and trundle a mop; nurse a baby, or turn a mangle; I can bind shoes, and make hay; milk a cow, or sing a psalm; and don't forget to say, that I'm a girl of strong moral perpensities.   [*Courtesies and exit*, L.

Mary. So, so; here's a discovery for the Bishop of Battersea! as my Harry calls Waxend. Oh, dear! I wish our marriage was over!—And yet, I'm sure, if Harry was to ask me, I should put it off for another year. Harry's to row for another wherry in a month. La! if he was to win that, as he did the last!—that might alter affairs.— Mr. and Mrs. Halliyard, with two boats of their own!— I'd have one, with a white awning all fringed round, and a flag at the stern, for Richmond parties, and 'tother for every-day work—Joe should row that. I like Joe, because he's Harry's friend, and he's so good-natured and poetical, and because he's so kind to me;—yes, he should row the every-day one, and my Harry should sit like a king in' the other; and then, when there happened to be no company, he should just pull me and the little ones down to——La! what am I thinking of? We've neither got the boat nor the little ones yet.

Joe. [*Singing without.*]

"Poll, dang it! how d'ye do?" &c.

Enter JOE TILLER, L. D. F.

Joe. Ah, my pretty Mary! I've been longing all the day to have a peep at your blue eyes. Why, what's the matter?

Mary. [*Pouting.*] I don't like your singing about Poll this, and Poll that. My name's Mary.

Joe. (c.) I mean no disrespect, Mary; but ar'n't you called Pretty Poll of Putney?

Mary. (L. c.) Oh, yes; and there's a parrot at the public-house—she calls herself Pretty Poll of the King's Arms.

Joe. Well, well, forgive me.

Oh, kill not my heart with a frown from your eyes,
For if you look angry, the poor flutterer dies.
Men may talk as they like, each pretends he's a wise 'un,—
A frown from a woman to true love is pison.

Mary. [*Mildly.*] Well, I'm sure I don't frown—I'm not angry, Joe; only, you see, Harry is in a fair way to be a most respectable proprietor of boats; and he wouldn't like his wife to be called Poll Halliyard this, and Poll Halliyard that. Decent people must have decent comportment.

Joe. Very true, Mary; every word you say is wisdom:

There's some folks speaks wisdom and sense every minute,
Some, when they opens their mouth, always puts their foot in it.

But here, Mary, I've brought you a present. [*Taking a ring from a paper.*] Here's a ring—a keeper: when Harry gives you a plainer ring, but of more value—ha!—then, Mary, put this on—his friend's present as a guard to protect his own. Harry loves you dearly, Mary, but not more than Joe loves you—as—as a friend.

Mary. Yes, Joe, I know you do; and I'll wear your ring, and dance with you at our wedding.

Joe. Will you, though?

Harry Halliyard. [*Without,* L. D. F.] Yo ho! the pretty Mary, there!

Mary. Oh, here he comes! [*Imitating.*] Yo ho! there, the saucy Harry! yo ho!

Harry. [*Without.*] Yo ho!—Now, a long pull, old one!

Joe. I forgot to tell you—don't be alarmed—Harry sent me forward that you mightn't be alarmed,—but poor old Sculler——

Mary. What—what of the old man?

Joe. Is going—to—to prison.

Mary. To prison!

Enter HARRY HALLIYARD, L. D. F.

Mary. [*Running to him.*] Oh, Harry! the old man— my dear Harry——

Enter OLD SCULLER, L. D. F.

Ha! [*Rushing to Sculler, and embracing him.*] You are not gone, then! What—what is the meaning of this?

Enter BLACK BRANDON, SAM SNATCHEM, *and several Watermen,* L. D. F.

What men are those? Is it true? is it true?

Harry. (c.) Come, cheer up, lass!—Why, you're as troubled as Chelsea Reach in a gale. Only shipped a little of the bilge water of misfortune : you and I must lend him a hand to bale him dry. Hark ye, lass—come here.

[*They retire up,* R.

Sna. (L.) [*To Brandon.*] She's a pretty little 'un, an't she?

Bra. (L. c.) Silence!

Sna. Got a nice little vaist, and a neat article of a foot; not like a pick-axe—as much behind as before.

Bra. Fool! hold your tongue!

Harry. [*Coming forward with Mary.*] Go and fetch it, then, Mary—will you?—There a little queen; and I'll talk a bit to these visitors. [*Exit Mary,* R.] Come, old heart, we're on the right tack; now just listen to me.— [*Crossing to and eyeing Brandon, who meets his gaze with ferocious defiance.*] Hark ye, my black-looking friend, it strikes me that, after all, you're a sort of a kind of a pirate. The paper you've brought is right, but how the devil did you run foul of it? Come, show your reckoning, as they say at sea. Who are you?

Bra. Who am I? I am one who thinks the frog of the river look's well when he questions the shark of the sea.

Harry. That observation's true in your log—shark, indeed; but when we get the shark in the shallows, let him look out.

Bra. [*Significantly.*] The frog would look pretty in the Atlantic.—I never forget an insult.

Harry. Tell us how I may insult a callous heart like yours, and I'll do it, that your memory may last for ever. [*Looking off*, R.] Ah! here comes the best girl in the world, with a load of ammunition that shall founder your cockle-shell.

Enter MARY, R., *with a canvass bag.*

Give it me, my lass. Look at that girl: she's life and all the world to me; even your iron soul must tell you I'm a happy fellow, for she loves me. Bless her blue eyes! they are heavens' stars to me.

Mary. (R. c.) Harry—Harry! remember——

Harry. (c.) I must talk to'em, lass; and just now my heart feels like a member of Parliament—it could speechify till a dissolution; but, hang it, girl, I hope to more purpose. [*To Brandon.*] Well, as I say, we love each other; we were both poor; I won a wherry; it enabled me to earn and to save money; she worked hard, too; we agreed to marry when we had saved thirty pounds; there's the sum. [*Throwing the bag at the feet of Brandon.*] Your debt is thirty-two: will you take it?—No!—There's the black demon of avarice grinning in every wrinkle of your ugly phis-og. But there, sir, [*Throwing down another bag.*] I have earned a pound to-day—that makes thirty-one; and if you don't take that, and discharge the old man, damme, I'll give you both a pounds' worth of drubbing to get a full receipt. [*Throwing off his jacket.*

Mary. [*Interposing.*] Stay, Harry, stay! It were a pity a humble and honest man should ever foul his hands by a contest with either a tyrant or a rogue. I don't mean to say, sir, you are the one or the other; but there's another pound, earned by honest labour: take your full demand, and quit the house, before this gallant spirit [*Pointing to Harry.*] bursts through the bonds of prudence, and makes you do it by the window.

Bra. [*Taking up the money, and laying down the paper.*] This is all I want; you can talk about honesty when I'm gone: it's not a saleable commodity, and I know nothing about it. But hark you, sir, [*Turning fiercely to Harry.*]—I've already told you I never forget an insult: we shall meet again. [*To Snatchem.*] Come, sir.

Sna. She's a werry pretty one, for all that, though there is a bit of the brimstone, too.

[*Harry turns, and moves towards him—he darts off*, R. D. F.

Harry. Why, old man, the tears are in your eyes; give us your hand; Poll and I have only to wait another year or two, and you are happy.

Scu. But I have prevented your being so.

Joe. Pshaw, never mind that; Harry, you're a noble fellow—Mary, you're a queen. I'll help you, I'll never go to the Crown and Crozier; but every farthing I can save, you shall have; we'll soon have the thirty pounds.

"" With a long pull and a strong pull, we'll shoot the bridge in stile,
And we'll have the thirty pounds, yet be merry all the while.''

Harry. What a happy man I am, old heart, though the shark has sheered off with the gold. Hang the mopusses! —what care I for the world's ups and downs, while I've my Poll and my Partner Joe?

Scu. You were made for each other, and I am the cause of a continued separation.

Mary. Not so; the money we have paid was Harry's, my earnings were trifling; and I love him more for sacrificing the means of our marriage, than I did for earning them; for that sacrifice was made for you, my second father. [*Turning to Harry.*] Why should we not struggle as well together as man and wife, as singly; if you think my hand a reward for your noble devotion, take it—I will be yours, even to-morrow.

Harry. [*Mad with joy, and kissing her.*] Eh, what, mine—to-morrow—my dear Mary: run, Joe, run down to Tommy Teazepsalm, the parish clerk; tell him I'm to be married to-morrow—run, old man, run to Will Wall-it, tell him to send me in a store of grog, we'll be merry to-night, my dear Mary; bless that fellow's black-looking ugly mug, if he hadn't come, I shouldn't—oh, my eyes, married to-morrow; Mary mine—what will old Dame say; married to-morrow; cut and run; my dear Mary—bear a hand, bear a hand.   [*Exit in ecstasies*, R. D. F.

SCENE III.—*Outside of Harry's House, with a Garden looking over the River—the opposite shore seen—boats passing—oars leaning against the door, &c.*

DAME HALLIYARD *discovered, busied spreading a table, near* R. S. E.—WATCHFUL WAXEND *seated on a stool near the table, smoking.*

Dame. (R.) And so Harry said I was to welcome some friends.

Wax. (R. C.) Yea, welcome them with a joyous spirit.

[*Drinking*.] I feel that thou hast made me welcome; I should like a little heeltap, a little more wax on the thread.
[*Offering the glass.*

Dame. [*Rising*.] You shall have it, though you're rather shaky now.

Wax. [*Rising, and coming forward*, c.] The struggling of the spirit is mighty within me; I want to preach, and I can't, till I've finished my pipe.

Dame. And so, my boy (bless him) is going to have a merry-making; well, well, I suppose Mary and he have made up the match : some mothers wouldn't like a young wife coming home, and turning them out of office, but I know the wench—a better doesn't breathe by the old river.

Wax. Ah, women are troublesome spirits.

Dame. What do you mean? you never suffered by them.

Wax. Haven't I, though; their love has been my ruin; I looked too much after the flesh; I worked very hard at my trade; but I couldn't help leaving a few wax ends about.

Dame. Pooh, you should have got married, as my Harry means to do: there's everything ready for him; there's his pipe, and Mary's favourite mug, and old Sam Sculler's backey-box. Oh, what a happy old woman I am to have two such children.

Harry. [*Without*, L. U. E.] Mother—Dame Halliyard —hoy, there!

Dame. Here they come.

Enter HARRY, MARY, JOE, OLD SAM SCULLER, *and* Watermen, L. U. E.

Oh, my dear boy, welcome all of you; Mary, my lass, give us a buss : well—Eh, where is it to be? Have you agreed—Um! can I have a new cap made? Hark ye, old Sam, you and I'll dance a gig at the wedding.

Scu. That we will, old lass; ah, you don't know.

Dame. Why, what's the matter?

Scu. Come here. [*They go up*, c.

Harry. Well, Mary, here's my Lord Bishop, all ready to marry us. How does your reverence feel to-day? Is the spirit strong within you—for we've news, news that will shake it. [*Waxend, very drunk, looking at his glass.*] Thanks to your good mother, its pretty strong; I had it waxed a little more.

Mary (R. C.) Master Watchful, were you ever in love?

Wax. (R.) Twenty-seven times.

Mary. Oh, shameful.

Harry. (c.) Do you know a place called Bullock Smithy ?

Wax. [*Staggered.*] I've heard of it.

Joe. Were you ever in love there ?

Wax. The spirit was strong.

Harry. Did a girl ever swear—

Wax. [*Interrupting.*] Don't mention it.

Harry. A girl from Bullock Smithy is here.

Wax. [*Alarmed.*] Here—then must I fly.

Joe. But she will see you.

Wax. She shan't—it's not mine ; mine are like wax-dolls, with hair like bristles, and eyes as sharp as an awl. I'll fly—I'll not be made a victim ; one more sup [*Drinking.*] and I'll exile myself as far as Tuttle Street ; farewell, Battersea—I'll—I'll not be sacrificed.

> [*Staggers off in great terror,* R.*—they all laugh— Dame Halliyard and Sculler come forward.*

Dame. Boy, you've done a noble action ; hang the pence, Mary and I will soon save it up again ; there's a grunter yet in the sty ; the wherry's tight and light ; you are strong and willing, and Mary's active and industrious. As for me, I shan't, I suppose, be able to reckon much on myself after a little time. Baby's clothes are tedious things for an old woman—Eh, boy ; eh, Mary. [*Laughing.*] Ha ! ha ! ha !

Harry. Come, let us be merry ; take a seat, dad. [*They all sit round the table.*] Joe, run yourself ashore ; Mary and I moor together. Mother, what matters it which way the wind blows, so that our hearts are true, and we have no leaks in our conscience ; fill out a bumper— let's drink a health to Mary—I'm so happy we're to be married to-morrow.

Dame. Fill, fill—I'll drink that—I'll drink that.

> [*While they are busy regaling, a boat rolls on,* L. U. E.*, filled with sailors.*

Enter BEN BOWSE *and Pressgang, landing quietly from the boat—*BLACK BRANDON *comes forward.*

Bra. [*Pointing to Harry.*] Those are the men—fine young fellows. [*Retires.*

Bowse. Aye, aye.

> [*The sailors approach silently—Harry snatches a kiss from Mary—raises his glass, and is about to drink her health, when Bowse taps him on the shoulder.*

Bowse. You must come with me.

Harry. [*Rising.*] Who are you?

Bowse. The king wants men.

Harry. What do you mean?

Bowse. You'll make a devilish good sailor, and must serve him.

Harry & Joe. Pressed!

Mary. Pressed!—Oh! no, no!

Bowse (R.) He'll come back an officer, my girl; and he'll have his friend with him.

Joe. (L. C.) No, you're out of your reckoning there. [*Crossing to Bowse.*] I serve a fire-office—here's my protection.

Bowse. [*Looking at the paper.*] All's right—you're safe.

Mary (R. C.) And must he go! oh, sir, for pity——

Bowse. Pity ar'n't among the articles of the press service, my pretty dear.

Harry. Right. Fiends incapable of pity first gave birth to the idea, and by fiends only is it advocated. What! force a man from his happy home, to defend a country whose laws deprive him of his liberty? But I must submit; yet, oh! proud lordlings and rulers of the land! do ye think my arm will fall as heavily on the foe as though I were a volunteer? No!—I shall strike for the hearts I leave weeping for my absence, without one thought of the green hills or the flowing rivers of a country that treats me as a slave!

Bowse. Duty is duty, and must be done.

Joe. So says the thief when he serves the devil,
And does it the readler 'cause it is evil.

Harry. Come, Mary, lass, [*She is almost fainting.*] cheer up; I'll return an admiral—be faithful to you in every clime. This little lock of hair shall be the sheet-anchor of our constancy. Bless you, mother! I must go.

Dame. [*Drying her tears, and stifling her sobs.*] You must, boy. I know you will do your duty as a man; but for the sake of the young lass, and for the old lass, too, don't be rash, my Harry: be a hero—I know you will. God bless you!

Harry. (C.) Dear mother!—Mary, bid me good bye—a kiss, lass!—You will be true to me? [*Mary points upwards.*] All's over.—I'm ready, lads.—Joe, you are my friend: take care of the wherry—protect Mary and my mother—be to them as I would! God bless you, Mary! [*Kissing her.*] I have your promise, Joe?

Joe. You have.

Harry. [*Wringing his hand.*] Farewell!—Mother— Mary! God bless you all!

Enter BLACK BRANDON, R.

Bra. [*To Bowse.*] Seize him! [*To Harry, sneeringly.*] You see I never forget an insult!
Harry. Ah, villain! art thou here?
[*He darts fiercely at Brandon, when he is dragged away, and the act drop falls—picture.*

END OF ACT I.

*** *A period of four years is supposed to elapse between the first and second act.*

ACT II.

SCENE I.—*The Quarter-Deck of the Polyphemus.*

Enter CAPTAIN OAKHEART, LIEUTENANT MANLY, *and* OFFICERS, *from the cabin,* R. D. F.

Oak. (c.) Gentlemen, the duty, for the performance of which we are assembled, though a painful, is an imperative one. To preserve the necessary discipline, we are compelled to reprimand a brave man for an act that confers honour on the British flag; yet, while obliged to condemn, we shall applaud and honour in our hearts,—one of the best seamen that ever trod a plank—one of the most fearless spirits that ever handled a cutlass,—his very courage must be restricted with severity, or his example and extraordinary success will banish subordination from the fleet.

Enter a MIDSHIPMAN, L., *with a Guard of Marines, conducting* HARRY HALLIYARD, *prisoner—he bows respectfully to the Officers.*

Oak. You have been four years aboard the Polyphemus?
Harry. (L. C.) Aye, your honour.
Oak. You were a volunteer?
Harry. No, your honour; I was a pressed man, pressed on the day before I was to be married to the prettiest and best lass in the world.
[*Taking a lock of hair out of his bosom, and kissing it.*
Oak. (R. C.) You are a brave fellow, Halliyard?

Harry. (L. c.) Thank your honour : there's no scarcity of 'em aboard this craft.

Oak. Right : I am proud of my crew, but brave men should never forget obedieuce to their superiors.. You have forgotten your duty ; you have been promoted since you came on board ; you are a petty officer, and Mr. Manly has ever been your friend ; yet you have proved yourself ungrateful.

Harry. Oh, your honour ! don't say that—it cuts me to the soul ! Do you think I can ever forget that Mr. Manly did all that he could to get me my pretty Poll's letter that was laying for me at Trieste, when we were up the Mediterranean ?—And he would have got it, too, but sudden orders came for us to join the fleet in the West Ingees.— My log wouldn't be worth keeping, if I hadn't got that in large letters. And then your honour's been so kind to me since I've been aboard, that you've almost made me forget the cruel law that took me from a young bride : so, what with your goodness, and the ship (bless her !) being called the Polly—Polyphemus, keeping me always in mind of somebody at home, I've begun to be almost happy.— Ingratitude ! May I spring a leak, and go down in the black sea of contempt, if ever I take such a villainous cargo on board !

Oak. And yet, Halliyard, you have dared to disobey orders. Mr. Manly, state your charges against him.

Man. (R.) I must first preface, that, in thus complaining of him, I am performing an imperative duty, with which no private feeling dare to interfere. He will respect me the more for a conscientious discharge of it, when I publicly avow that he has twice saved my life.

Harry. Oh, your honour ! say no more of that. I'd have done it even for sulky Sam, the cook's mate, though he is the most disagreeable swab in the whole crew.

Oak. Proceed, Manly, with your charges.

Man. After orders had been past to lie close, (we having in the night crept in, and anchored under the enemy's guns), he secretly persuaded twelve of the crew to a breach of discipline. They lowered themselves over the side into the ship's boat, and, at the imminent hazard of the lives of all, and the destruction of the commodore's plans, they attempted the cutting out of an armed store-ship, loaded with ammunition and supplies.

Harry. Avast there, your honour ! There's a bit of an error in your charge. We *did* cut her out, and brought

c

her clear off, in spite of the fire of all their batteries, and
the bellowing and blazing of their flotilla to boot; and if
your honour only remembers the prisoners we brought in—
there were just two to a man—six-and-twenty Spaniards,
and we without a scratch, excepting Georgy Gunnel, who
would be so venturesome as to fight six——

Oak. Still you were wrong.

Harry. Wrong! your honour. Begging your honour's
pardon, a great deal of it was your own fault.

Oak. Mine?

Harry. Aye, your honour, with respect be it spoken.—
Don't you remember when you had me on the quarter,—to
give me a little jobation, because, in the action of the day
before, I took the trouble to go and fetch the Frenchman's
flag, to tie round Mr. Manly's wound—don't you remember that, as I was standing by, you pointed out where the
store-ship lay, and said it would be a glorious thing to dis-
appoint the enemy of all the powder and stores on board?
Ah, I see your honour recollects; and you said, too, it
was an impossibility. Now comes my fault. Says I to
myself, I don't think so; I knows about a dozen as would
do it, and, as our chaplain says, damme! if I don't try.
And so I axed 'em, and they said yes; and we tried it, and
we did it; and that's all I can say about it, your honour.

Oak. Now mark what might have been the consequence
had you failed. We were in the presence of an enemy of
superior strength; the policy of the commodore was to
hem them with their heavy vessels in shore; day by day
we had been creeping on them, till, on the night in question, we had taken up a position, which, with every advantage on our side, must have brought them to a battle.—
Now, as I before observed, had you failed, our resources
and position would have been known, and the prospects of
the war totally destroyed in consequence.

Harry. But as it was, your honour, they thought the
devil was among them, and, standing at all hazards out to
sea, dropped like pigeons into the commodore's hands.—
Your honour will admit that, although you punish the
cause——

Enter a MIDSHIPMAN, L.

Mid. Sail on the larboard quarter, your honour.

Oak. What is she?

Mid. Can't yet make her out. [*They all listen eagerly.*

Oak. Jump aloft, Halliyard; take my glass; you've a
quick eye—report her build.

Harry. I'm a prisoner, your honour.

Oak. We'll take your parole for the present.

Harry. [*Going.*] Thank your honour. [*Returning.*] I suppose, your honour, I mustn't board this craft, whatever she is, till—till I can lay my grappling irons on her.

[*Exit, bowing,* L.

Oak. Gentlemen, each to his quarters; we will resume when this business is over.

Re-enter MIDSHIPMAN, L.

Mid. Halliyard reports a brig, armed—black hull—a good sailor—no colours.

Oak. My life on it, he is right. Be brisk, gentlemen; we may have warm work in store: to your quarters—quick! quick!

[*Exeunt,* R. D. F.—*Shouts from forward, &c.*

SCENE II.—*Between Decks of a Slave Ship—the ports open—the hatchway seen,* C.—*a large cask,* L.

Slaves discovered chained to the floor—a Seaman walking to and fro, heavily armed, and carrying a whip—other Seamen hastily passing with powder, &c. — BLACK BRANDON, *with a glass, at the port.*

Bra. (R.) Curses on her! she walks the water like a witch! Are all the black cattle safe aboard?

Sea. Aye, aye.

Bra. Where, in the name of the fiend, is Bowse? She keeps the weather gage in spite of us; and yet the Black Bet is no skulker on a wind. Hark ye, ye nigger animals, if I hear the least noise, or see the least sign of grumbling among ye, I'll make sharks' meat of every devil of you!—[*Looking out of the port with his glass.*] Her sails rise above the waters as fast as the cloud of a white squall.

Enter ZINGA *from the hold,* C., *heavily manacled—he creeps close to Brandon, and falls on his knees.*

What the devil do you want?

Zin. (C.) I would ask mercy, master: poor Zinga begs his wife.

Bra. (R.) Your wife, fool!—She's in my cabin: had she been kinder, you might now have had your arms and legs at liberty.

Zin. I'll wear your fetters, master; see—they eat into my flesh; yet I will be happy: let me have my wife—my Zamba!

c 2

Bra. You thought to escape me, did you?

Zin. I followed but the impulses of nature. Three years ago you tore me from my country—from the presence of my parents, and the arms of the maid, who is now my wife; regardless of my shrieks and cries, you dragged me away to slavery; my heart was broken; and, if I murmured, the lash was my only answer. Yet, master, I did not seek revenge; I could have had it. Yes, one night, when you were sleeping, my knife was at your throat; but I thought of the words the good white man said to me at my own home, when he taught us his religion, and I conquered the temptation. Well, I served you faithfully; you again sought my country to make more slaves; I fled to join my Zamba. Was it a crime? Oh! give her to me, and I will be your slave for ever! In pity to my agony, spare her! give her to my arms unharmed!

Bra. [*Striking him.*] Back, beast!

  [*Zinga staggers, then making a weapon of his chain,*
  he rushes to strike Brandon, who presents his sword
  —the Seaman draws a pistol, cocks it, and is about
  to fire.

Bra. [*Preventing him.*] Stop!—If we throw him overboard, his carcass may betray us to those bull-dogs. Give him the whip, and keep an eye upon him. Let us get clear of this hell-cat in chase, and his hours are numbered.

  [*The Seaman strikes Zinga with the whip, till, over-*
  come by pain, he crouches piteously at the feet of
  Brandon, who fells him with a blow—Brandon
  bursts into a loud laugh, while the Seaman thrusts
  Zinga among the rest of the Slaves.

Enter BEN BOWSE, *with a glass in his hand,* L. S. E.

Bra. What news?

Bowse. I've made her out, though her hull isn't above the water, for I know the cut of her jib. 'Tis the Polyphemus sloop; she that I was boatswain of, and deserted from, when I fell in with you. We must make more way than we do now, or she'll walk over us: 'tis the fastest craft in the service.

Bra. [*Looking out.*] She's a flying devil! [*Distant report of a gun heard.*] Boom!—She's began to talk: we must lighten the Bet. [*Gun.*] Boom again!—Ah! chatter away!—If we can keep out of the reach of her long speechifyers for another hour, we may double her in the dark.— Some of our heavy metal must go over.   [*Exit,* R.

Bowse. It'll be all of no use, Master Brandon. [*Looking out.*] See, her sails flap—she is about to take a longer reach. [*Gun.*

Enter WATCHFUL WAXEND, R. S. E., *his dress half-sailor, half-cobbler.*

Wax. Oh, lord! oh, lord! I wish I was at Battersea! I'd better have fathered all the children of Bullock-Smithy, than been kidnapped here, and treated like a white nigger; and now I shall be shot at like a piece of wax stuck in the middle of a target!
[*A shout and noise heard on the deck.*

Bowse. There goes Black Tommy overboard.

Wax. [*To the Negroes.*] Oh, Lord! they'll be coming down for some of your black Tommy's soon.
[*Shouts and noise again.*

Bowse. There goes his brother Bill.

Wax. My spirit sinks; when they've settled all the bills they will dot and carry one with me. Oh, Mr. Bowse, who is it they are throwing overboard—how many is there before it comes to my turn.

Bowse. Pshaw, fool! it's the two guns, our heavy thirty-two pounders. Ha! she feels it, but not enough. [*Noise again.*] Right, Brandon, better lose our metal than our lives.

Wax. Very right, I'll lose anything rather than my life. [*Gun.*

Enter BLACK BRANDON, *hastily*, R. S. E.

Bra. She nears us fast; will it never be night; curses on her. I've ordered Rasper to cut eight inches into her ribs; let her shake a bit, so that we can run under the rock of Martinique—damn the repairs. [*Looking out.*

Wax. Oh! if he was to cut eight inches into my ribs!

Bra. Bravo, Bet! she'll bother them yet. [*Crash heard, followed by a gun.*] It's all over with us! no, curse it, no—the black cattle shall feed the fishes first, every mother's son of them. Ah! hark ye, Bowse, do you take charge of the papers; tie a shot to them, and if we're spoke to, let the fishes read 'em. [*Crash and gun.*]

Enter a SAILOR, L. S. E.

What now?

Sai. They've carried away the quarter bulwarks—shall we heave to?

Bra. The first man that speaks of surrender, I'll scat-
ter his brains about the deck.   [*Exit sailor, L.*

Wax. I'll hide myself, for I'm sure to speak of it.

[*Gets into the cask, and stoops down to conceal himself.*

Bra. Stay, a thought strikes me; its getting dark,
pick me out one of those niggers—we'll give him a floating-
bath; if they shorten sail to pick him up, we gain time;
if they don't, the sharks will get him.

Wax. [*Peeping out of the cask.*] Oh, Lord! they'll be
mistaking me for a nigger.

Bra. Bowse, I have it; bring me the woman from my
cabin.   [*Exit Bowse, L.*

Zin. [*Darting forward, and kneeling.*] Master, you will
give me my wife—oh, master, mercy, master!

Bra. [*Laughing.*] Ay, ay!

Zin. [*Mad with joy.*] Master, good master!

Enter Sailors, with ZAMBA, *L.—she rushes into the arms
of Zimba.*

Bra. Tear them asunder!   [*The Sailors separate them.*

Zin. [*Piteously.*] No, no; you mistake: master captain has given me my dear wife, my own Zamba; master
will make Zinga happy.

Bra. Tie her in an empty hogshead; let her gently over
the side; they'll hear her shrieks.

[*They seize her—she screams—Zinga breaks from the
Sailors and embraces her—she is dragged off, Zinga
clinging to her, and shrieking—he is pulled back by
the Sailors.*

Zin. [*Turning to Brandon.*] You are a white man, can
your own God forgive you?

[*Falls fainting—Brandon looks out, L.*

Enter BEN BOWSE, L. S. E., *with papers—shrieks as of
Zamba heard in the shouts—they grow fainter and
fainter as she is seen through the port-holes floating
away—they listen.*

Bra. 'Tis done.

Bowse. 'Tis a bad act.

Bra. 'Tis good policy; see, they shorten sail to pick
her up. Now's our time; one or two more, and we defy
them. Are all the papers there?

Bowse. They are.

Bra. We gain upon them; yes, they are changing their
course to snap at my black bait: I'll upon deck; have the

husband ready for the gudgeons, and, d'ye hear, if it comes
to the worst, you know what to do with the papers.

Bowse. Ay, ay. [*Exit Brandon, R.—Bowse runs and
looks out.*] All right, the poor thing will be saved—ah,
them Poly=phemus lads are of the right sort ; what a fool
have I been to leave her—no matter, I musn't live to be
found out.

Zin. [*Recovering from his swoon, and rushing to the
port.*] Ha, she is there ! I see her arms raised for help,
and as the wind comes I hear her wild shrieks—my brain
will burst.   Ha ! the ship is shortening sail—they put out
a boat—they near her—one moment more and—oh,
misery ! the cask is filling—they will be too late—my eyes
will start—she sinks—she is lost !—no, no ; a sailor plunges
into the waves ; I cannot see them now ; yes, he rises ;
she is in his arms ; they take her into the boat. [*Rushing
forward, and falling on his knees.*] She is saved ! thank
God ! thanks ! thanks !

   [*A momentary pause—a terrific crash heard—a report
   of cannon, and then a loud shout and lamentations.
   —Part of a sail drops before the ports, and gives
   the effect of the vessel being violently shaken.*

Bowse. [*Tying the papers to a ball, and laying them near
the hatches.*] The game's up ; they've shot away her mast.
[*Exit with the Sailors, rushing off as if to go upon deck.*

Wax. [*Creeping out of the cask.*] Oh, lord, how hot I
am ! my flesh melteth and my spirit waxeth faint ; they've
shot away the mast, I wish they had shot away the master.
[*Guns.*] There, they're at it again ;—what a row they're
kicking up about these papers—they seem of consequence ;
I'll take one or two for my own private reading when
I'm at home at Battersea—don't mention Battersea, I'm
likely to be battered at sea, here.

   [*He takes out some of the papers and hides them in
   his bosom—gun, and noise.*

Re-enter BOWSE, hastsly, L. S. E.

Bowse. It's all over ; another minute, and they'll board
us. [*Snatching up the papers and throwing them through
the port into the sea..*] Now, then, to die like a man.
                                                [*Exit, R.*

Wax. [*Hiding in the barrel.*] Now, then, to live like a
man. [*Guns—crash.*] There seems to be a deal of welting
going on ; I hope one side will get leathered.   Oh, Bullock-Smithy, Battersea, any where but here.

[*Music.—Noise continued—Sailors cross hurriedly—
Zinga rises, looks round, and tries in vain to force
his chains—the Polyphemus is seen through the
ports of the Black Bess—a tremendous crush heard
—loud shouts firing and clashing of swords.*

Enter Slavers with Sailors of the Polyphemus fighting—
BOWSE *and* MANLY, HARRY *and* BRANDON.—*Bowse is
disarmed after a furious conflict, and, rushing past
desperately, jumps through the port into the sea.—
Brandon is cut down by Harry, who turns from him,
when Brandon fires a pistol, which knocks off his hat.*

Harry. [*Turning upon him.*] Missed, you black-looking
piratical robber! you'll swing for this. [*To Captain Manly,
pointing to the Negroes.*] There, your honour, there they
are, poor souls, chained all of a row like so many bullocks
at Smithfield. [*Pointing his sword at Brandon.*] May six
of my week days be banyan days, if I ar'nt as great a mind
to let your ugly soul adrift on its downward voyage as—
but no, I'll leave you to the gallows.

Man. Let the hold be searched, and the manacles struck
off these poor creatures.

[*Harry goes to the hatchway and looks down, while
the Sailors are releasing the Slaves.—Black Brandon, making an effort, rises, and with a small dirk
is about to stab Harry in the back, when Waxend,
peeping from the barrel, snatches a pistol from
the belt of a Sailor who is passing, and shoots him
in the head—Brandon shrieks and falls,* R.

Wax. [*Looking knowingly from the cask.*] There's a
ball of wax for you, my boy.

[*He jumps out of the cask, and runs into the corner,
L., as if afraid of the pistol he has fired—Harry
turns his head, and looks significantly at Brandon.*

Bra. [*Raising himself.*] It's all over—run down at last
by a Peter-boat!—Well, well! no hanging this time!—
Hallyard, you don't recollect me; but I remember you!
I never forget an insult!

Harry. [*Approaching him.*] I recollect that voice—
those words! [*Recognising him.*] Is it possible?

Bra. Ay, ay; I did a good thing in getting you pressed
—made a neat rod for my own hide.   Well, it's all over—
the Black Bet and her captain will go to Davy Jones together; put me over to the sharks—Ha! ha!—I never forget
an insult! [*Hysterically.*] Ha, ha, ha!   [*Dies.*

Man. Let the ship be cleared of the dead—turn all hands upon deck.

Harry. But the poor woman, your honour, that we picked up, she may have a friend or a brother among these ebony gentlemen.

Man. Right : pass the word for the negro woman.

    [*Music.—Zamba's voice is heard without*, R.

Zin. [*Coming forward and looking anxiously at Harry.*] Zamba l my wife l

Harry. [*Eagerly.*] Your wife ?

  [*Zinga nods assent—Harry rushes off,* R.—*re-enters with Zamba, and throws her into the arms of her husband.—In an ecstasy of gratitude, they prostrate themselves at the feet of Manly and Harry.*

Harry. Lord love my eyes, the poor creturs are lovyers— she's the Poll of his heart; tip us your black fin, my honest fellow; there's one at home I'd give the world to hug in my arms as you do your brown fair one here.— Here's a bit of her silky hair—it's my breast-plate in the day of battle, and my library of comfort in the dark hours of the night-watch.

Man. Hallyard, I shall leave you as prize-master while I return to report to the captain. [*Introducing Waxend.*] This poor fellow saved your life—you must look to him. Come, bear a-hand, lads.   [*Exit,* R.

Harry. Ay, ay, your honour. [*To Waxend.*] Follow me, my lad, we'll overhaul your log. [*To the Sailors.*] And, do you hear, boys, let the wounded be looked to—let the poor niggers go free upon deck. Dance, you black angels, no more captivity, the British flag flies over your head, and the very rustling of its folds knocks every fetter from the limbs of the poor slave.   [*Exit,* R.

SCENE III.—*Cabin of the Slaver.*

Enter HARRY HALLYARD, *followed by* WATCHFUL
WAXEND, R.

Harry. (L. C.) Now, my lads, who are you—you saved my life, and I thank you ; I'll do the same for you another time ; but—why, there's a something about the build of your figure-head as strikes me—did you ever cross my latitude afore ?

Wax. (C.) I don't know what you mean by your latitude, but I've crossed your door-way at Battersea many a time to see the old dame—capital punch she used to make —hav'n't had a drop since.

Harry. Why, surely, no—it can't be the bishop—what, Master Watchful Waxend turned pioneer and slaver !

Wax. I was a slave myself—they made a white nigger of me ; I was kidnapped on board one night when the spirit had mastered me, and I fell asleep at Wapping, and I've had nothing but whopping ever since.

Harry. Give us your hand, it does one's heart good to see any one from the dear home.   Well, and how was my Poll, pretty and constant, eh ? and the old lass, old mother, and Joe, eh ? how are they ? speak, lad, speak.

[*Shaking hands violently with Waxend.*

Wax. So I—I—I will when you've done joggling so.

Harry. Why don't you give fire, then ? my heart's up in my mouth ; my dear Mary ! [*Looking at the lock of hair.*] Let out a reef of your jawing tackle, my lord bishop, or you'll get monkey's allowance. [*Impatiently.*] How are they all ? how's Poll ?

Wax. I can't tell you, I've been away these three years.

Harry. Oh, lord ! oh, lord ! no news any way ; not one letter have I had, and I've wrote a dozen.

Wax. Oh, yes, stop a bit ; I've got one for you.

Harry. Eh, from Mary ? where is it, lad, where is it ? How did you get it ?

Wax. Why, she gave it me to take to the Admiralty the night before I was kidnapped ; I popped it into my portmantle, and stuck it in with a ball of wax, and so I've kept it ever since. [*Untieing his neckerchief, taking out the the letter, and giving it to Harry.*] Here it is.

Harry. [*Snatching and kissing it.*] Bless her little fingers L How it smells of cobbler's wax !—never mind— let's see what she says. [*Opening and reading it.*] " *My dearest, dear Harry,*" bless her ! " *we hav'n't none of us never had no letter from you*"—why, I'd writ a matter of four before this was writ, " *and I do nothing but cry for fear of some accident,*" bless her pretty eyes, my poor Mary ! " *Oh, Harry, you ar'n't unconstant, sure*"—I'll be damn'd if I am ! " *your poor old mother asks the letter-man every day whether he expects one from you to-morrow. Joe's very kind, and works like a good one for the old dame.*"   God bless him ! " *She's crying over my shoulder now. Do write—I can't see the paper—excuse blottings, my dear Harry—I must give over. My heart will break if you don't write—do, soon, my dear, dear own Harry, and God bless you.*—MARY MAYBUD. P. S.—*Mother's and Joe's love, and mine a million times.*" Thank you, lad, for bringing this; thank you, thank you; bless them all.

[*Sinks his head on Waxhead's shoulder, and weeps.*

Wax. Why, Harry, Harry.

Harry. Oh, I ar'n't ashamed of these drops; when the heart's brim full of love and happiness, it must run over somewhere, and where and why shouldn't it at the eyes?—I don't think a man has less fire and courage in him for having a little of the water of affection. [*Crossing to* R. C.

Wax. [*Giving Brandon's papers.*] Here's something may serve to brighten you up a bit; may serve, as I say, to put a little more wax on the thread.

Harry. [*Looking with ecstasy on the papers.*] Where! eh! what! correspondence with the enemy!—Umph—map of a secret cove or harbour beneath the Rock of Montinique,—plan of the communication with the fort—list of pirate signals—all's right.

Enter ZINGA, R. S. E.

Zin. (R.) It was you, sir, who saved my Zamba's life; I owe you my gratitude. The object dearest to your heart is glory—I can put the pirate's horde into your hands; I have been his messenger to the rock for near two years: do you prepare a strong cable by which you can ascend; put me ashore; I will enter the fort as if from him; I will lower a rope from above, and—you understand?

Harry. I do, my brave fellow; the rock's ours; you shall be made a general for this, and [*Turning to Waxend.*] you an archbishop; not a moment must be lost—we are right off the rock now; the enemy will know this vessel; here we have the signals, and let British courage do the rest, huzza! Dam'me, I'll plant the British flag on their fort before the moon sinks. Bear a-head, lads; old England for ever! [*Exeunt,* R. S. E.

SCENE IV.—*Moonlight—The Slavers Fort and Stronghold on a high rock at the back,* L., *approached by a flight of steps cut out of the rock—a Rampart running across from the steps to* R. S. E.—*a pole on the rampart with a lamp near the bottom, with a cord attached to it, the whole having the appearance of immense height.*

A SENTINEL *discovered patrolling, heavily armed.*

Sen. The Black Bet has taken a long sweep this time ;
it's my turn for a cruise next—better than being cooped
up in this dog-hole.   I thought I made her out this after-
noon ; if so, she'll be for running under the rock to-night.
Let me see, this is four hundred feet above the sea, yet I
can almost fancy I feel the spray. [*Yawning.*] Yaw, aw ;
and by the booming of the cave beneath, in spite of the
moon's smiling, I should say it will be a rough night.
Yaw—I'm devilish sleepy. [*A signal like a boatswain's call
is heard.*] What devil's bird is that chirriping ? [*The signal repeated twice—he runs and looks over the rampart.*]
'Tis Brandon—there's the signal light of the Black Bet
under the rock ; I must show the lamp for 'em to hoist the
portcullis in the path below. [*Raises the lamp by a cord
to the top of the pole.*] There's a wind rising, and Brandon's not the man to hug the shore.   We shall lose our
supplies. [*Yawning.*] Yaw—I'd rather turn in, than be
prowling here with a storm brewing—yaw.

> [*A knock heard,* L. S. E.—*he opens the door.*
>
> *Enter* ZINGA, L., *with a wallet.*

Oh, it's you, Master Nigger, is it ; well, what luck this
trip ?

Zin. Good, Master Beargruel, good.   Here, [*Giving a
bottle.*] here's a drop of the good ; drink, while I deliver
my message.

> [*Music, piano.—While the Sentinel drinks, Zinga
> draws a rope from his wallet and makes fast the end
> to a stauncheon, and drops it over the rock.*

Sen. (R. C.) I was as glad to see that light below as if
I'd had a fortune aboard.

Zin. [*Looking over the rampart.*] 'Tis a fearful height.

Sen. [*Still drinking.*] It is.

Zin. Hark how the wind howls. [*Aside.*] If their hearts
should fail—'tis too much for mortal courage to contemplate.

Sen. [*Turning to Zinga.*] Here's your bottle—yaw, aw.

Zin. No, keep it till my return.

Sen. Yaw—right. [*Exit Zinga,* L. S. E.] That black's
got a white soul.   I—I'm very sleepy ; another pull at the
bottle may wake me—[*Drinking.*] I wish I was aboard the
brig, [*Walking about hastily to keep awake.*] I—yaw, aw.
[*Laying down on the steps.*] Capital ; yes, I—yaw.

> [*Goes to sleep.*

Re-enter ZINGA, *cautiously*, L. S. E.

Zin. [*Watching.*] The opiate in the brandy has taken
effect; now to my task.

[*Music.—He pulls up the cord he had lowered, and
secures the cable which is attached to it with sticks
run through it, and fastens it securely to the staun-
cheon.—A pause.*

Zin. [*Stooping and looking anxiously over the rock.*] The
rope is pulled; they will make the attempt; 'tis a fearful
peril. I see by the torch in the boat which the preserver
of my Zamba holds, that they have begun to mount; he is
the last to cut off all retreat; each has his cutlass in his
mouth, and with a raging sea beneath them, five-and-
twenty souls are trusted to a single rope. The howling
wind below dashes them against the rock; I can gaze no
longer, my heart sickens at their danger, yet, like the
basilisk, it fascinates me to the spot. They pause—does
one heart shrink? the word is passed from man to man.
What do I see? Hallyard is mounting over the shoulders
of those above him; the wind almost extinguishes his
torch. Ha! he with his cutlass compels the men to
mount. Ha! they fall! no, 'tis but the torch; they are
in darkness—still they mount; should the rope give way—
it has worn with their weight upon the rock—should it
break—no, no! they are here.

[*Music.—Harry is seen on the cable waving the Union
Jack—he springs over the battlements followed by
Sailors, and shakes hands with Zinga, who points
to the Sentinel, whom one of the Sailors has raised
his sword to strike.,*

Harry. [*Preventing him.*] No, no, the poor fellow
sleeps; all fair and above board [*Securing the arms of
the Sentinel, and placing them against the rampart, then
trying the door of the fort.*] So fastened—perhaps this
fellow has the keys. [*Searching him.*] What's to be done
—I have it.

[*He shakes the Sentinel, and the Sailors retire,* R.

Sen. [*Waking.*] Hollo! who the devil are you?

Harry. Silence; I am from Brandon.

Sen. Oh, good; I'll inform Sebastian and the rest.

Harry. Do so.

*Music.—The Sentinel goes up the steps and gives three
knocks at the door of the fort—a guard puts his
head from above, the Sentinel gives the pass-word,*

D

*" Brandon and the Black Bet"—the Guard retires
—Harry motions his men forward—they range on
each side the door.*

Sen. [*To Harry.*] What does this mean ?

Harry. [*Seizing him, and putting a pistol to his head.*]
That you are in our power ; one word, and you die.

Sen. I don't fear death.

  [*The door is thrown open, and the Pirates rush out—
the Sentinel calls out "* Treachery!*" but too late—
Harry snatches up the Sentinel's fire-lock, and dis-
charges it at the Pirates—one of them is seen on
the top of the fort bearing a tri-coloured flag—the
Sailors dash into the fort—a general conflict en-
sues—a shell is thrown as if from the ship below
—it falls among the combatants—Harry seizes it
and hurls it into the fort—an explosion takes place
—the fort is blown up—torches are brought on—
Harry attacks and disarms the commandant, whom
he conquers—the Pirates are subdued—the fort
bursts into flames—Harry dashes through the fire,
rushes to the top of the fort, seizes the pirate with
the tri-coloured flag, hurls him into the sea, and
hoists the British standard, amidst enthusiastic
cheers.—Tableau.*

END OF ACT II.

ACT III.

SCENE I.—*The Interior of the Seamen's Friend Inn,
Portsmouth—a large bow window, c. f., through which
is seen the road and quay beyond, with the docks, vessels, &c.—a fire-place, r.—the bar, with a glass parti-
tion, through which the people are seen serving, l. 3d e.
—tables, forms, &c.—the church bells ringing.*

A Fidler *discovered on a high chair, r.—another outside
the window, in the street, playing different nautical
tunes.*

Sailors *and* Girls *dancing—other Sailors with their
Girls on their knees—some, intoxicated, sitting on the
ground, examining a Jew Duffer's slops and trinkets,
and buying handkerchiefs, with which they decorate the
girls—others they put in their pockets, which are imme-*

diately stolen, and re-sold to the Jews by the Girls—a party of Seamen, quite drunk, round the fire-place with a frying-pan and a pack of cards—they pour spirits into the pan, and, amidst uproarious laughter, fry the cards and their watches.

WATCHFUL WAXEND, *fresh rigged out as a Sailor, sitting c., with a girl on each knee, and a long pipe in his mouth.*

CHORUS OF SAILORS.

Sailors lead a jolly, jolly life,
While roving on the ocean;
In every port they have a wife,
Of every girl a notion.
Tol de rol, &c.

Wax. Yes, my loves, to be sure you shall have as much grog as you can swim in; but as for the rings and things you want, I'll give you them the next time we come to Portsmouth. [*The Girls get up, disappointed, and go to those Sailors who are buying of the Jews.*] Oh, dear! [*Rising.*] Yes, they'd soon bring the coblers all to an end. [*To a Sailor, who is frying his watch.*] Hollo, Jack! if you hadn't kept your watch better at sea, you wouldn't have been able to make so free with your time ashore.

Sailors. [*Laughing and shouting.*] Bravo! Bishop of Battersea!

Wax. Bishop of Battersea!—I wish I was at Battersea. But I've given up the bishop line now; it's a bad trade, and I'm anxious to mix in respectable society. [*All laugh.*] They cured me aboard the slaver of preaching: you see, none but the niggers would listen to me; and I thought it was all nonsense to preach to them as didn't understand; though, to be sure, there are some in the line who ar'n't fit to preach to them as I does. [*Turning to the Fidler.*] Come, strike up a tune, old Rosin! give me a hornpipe—common time.

A DANCE.

Harry Hallyard. [*Without, L.*] Yo! ho!

Enter HARRY HALLYARD, L.—*they all cheer him, and retire up, except Waxend.*

Harry. (L. C.) [*To Waxend.*] Yo! ho! lads!—Here I find you. Rather queerish anchorage, though, [*Pointing to the girls.*]—lots of rocks and quicksands—eh! [*Pointing to the Duffers.*] and swarming with sharks, too.

D 2

When I landed, I could have knelt down, but every one was looking ;—my heart kept tittuping—tittuping! and the tears of a whole lifetime seemed swelled into a large lump just here. So I pressed Mary's lock of hair, with the iron gripe of a seaman, to my heart ; crowded all sail ; and, without seeing a single landmark, made this harbour ; but how the devil I managed to steer clear of the chaiseses and the postesses, I'm jiggered if I can reckon.

Wax. (c.) I've seen two or three London-looking chaps about here ; and so I——

Harry. [*Eagerly.*] Eh ?—Did you ask 'em about Mary, and Joe, and the old house ?

Wax. I was just going to do it, when one of 'em says to the other, [*Mimicing.*] " Demme! what a orrid smell of tah !—I never could abide the wo-tah, demme !" So, you see, after that, I thought it was no use axing 'em about a waterman's home ; for their manners convinced me they were no better nor lords or linen-drapers, or some such people !

Harry. Well, well—have you made soundings about the coach ?

Wax. Aye, aye.

Harry. And secured the berths ?

Wax. Aye.

Harry. Then I'll only just beat about here till the captain bears down with a few gimcracks, that want stowage, and then crowd all sail for London. What's the name of the craft we're to go by ?

Wax. The Nonpareil.

Harry. The Nonpareil ! I wish it had been the Polly, or the Polly-phemus ; but never mind : the Nonpareil will answer for my Mary. So, do you hear ? heave a head, and just make a minute of the exact time they say they'll weigh anchor.

Wax. To be sure I will, and ask all about her rate of sailing : there's a fair wind—we shall soon be at Battersea.

[*Exit*, L.

Harry. I'm there now: I can see the old mother, with the bellows in her lap, listening to Mary, as she reads my last letter about coming home ; I can see the tears standing in the wrinkles of her dear old cheeks; and I can hear Mary's voice quivering a bit, as she comes to the part where I tell her that I love her more than ever ;—Joe, in the corner, with his pipe, fancying he's shaking hands with old friend, Harry, and puffing out the smoke to hide his quivering lips ;—I can see 'em all three, and the old wherry, and Sculler, picking gooseberries in the garden, and the old clock behind the door, ticking louder as if to welcome me: I can see 'em—I can hear 'em! What a· fool I am ! I'm crying like a boy !

Jew. [*Coming down,* L. C.] Von't you puy noting for de pretty tears ?

Harry. (C.) No, I'll buy nothing; I'll take her home no wishey-washey trinkum-trankums, no base metal covered with a little finery, like the ugly figure-head of the Saracen's phisog with a gold beard, but I'll take her the pure coin of an unaltered affection, and the hard earnings of five years of toil and glory.

Jew. Very nice, put you'd petter take dem de earrings or de shoe puckles, ma tear.

[*Goes up,* C., *and sits with the girls.*

Harry. Mary would give all the finery in the world for one word of love ; my eyes ! I'm so happy! my heart is as merry as a newly made middy, and I feel running before the wind of joy with all the sails of content filled to bursting.

Re-enter WATCHFUL WAXEND, L.

Wax. All right ! in half an hour they'll take the peg out of the last. Pooh! I mean to say, weigh anchor, or, vulgarly speaking, be ready to start in that time.

Harry. Hurrah ! eh—here, shipmates. [*The sailors and lasses come forward.*] Some of us have been five years together, let our parting be a merry one ; order some punch, I'll pay for all ; let us have a dance, drink success to our ship, and then home to our sweethearts and wives. [*Waxend orders liquor at the bar.*] The Polyphemus sloop! the pretty Polyphemus ! [*All shout and drink.*] (*Aside.*) The pretty Polly ! Fill again—I wish the. captain would bear down. Now, my lads, Captain Oakheart, and the memory of the brave Manly ! [*They drink.*

Enter CAPTAIN OAKHEART, L.—*they all shout.*

Oak. Thanks, my brave fellows; I'll give you a toast anon. Hallyard.

Harry. Your honour.

Oak. I shall see you in London soon ; if you call at my bankers you will find that your friend, Lieutenant Manly, has made you his heir ; you saved his life twice, Harry ! but your arm couldn't save him from the grim tyrant in

D 3

the last action, and as he had no relatives, you will now come into possession of three hundred a year.

Harry. Oh, gemini! three hundred a year! was there ever such a sum!

Oak. Don't let wealth spoil you and your pretty Poll, but tell her that your captain, who admires your honest integrity, will be her father on the day of marriage, and give her, too, the best protection—a good husband.

Harry. Oh, your honour, I'm all over gratitude! Won't Poll be proud, not of the money, though I thank and bless the good lieutenant for it! (heaven rest his brave soul!) but to think that your honour, a captain just posted, should— Oh! my heart, what a jolly day we will have!

Oak. Come, my lads! fill me a glass of punch! [*To Waxend.*] In the meantime, my good fellow, here is a purse of fifty guineas for the papers you furnished us in the slaver.

Wax. [*Taking the purse, and bowing awkwardly.*] Oh, thank your honour. [*Aside.*] My eye! won't I buy a stock of leather and wax.

[*Retires, c.—Harry gives Captain Oakheart a glass of punch.*

Oak. Here's our country, and may she always have sons as brave in battle, and as humane in victory, as the lads of the Polyphemus!   [*Drinking.*

> [*Great shouting without, during which Oakheart takes leave, and exits, R.*
> [*A coach is seen through the window, c. f.—people enter, L.—Harry and Waxend take leave, and exit, L.—they are seen through the window to mount the coach—the confusion recommences, the horn blowing, fiddling, &c.—a Sailor commences a hornpipe on the roof of the coach, which gives way, and he falls through amidst great laughter, hurrahing, and waving of hats, as the scene closes.*

SCENE II.—*Interior of Joe's House.*

Enter JOE TILLER, *with his jacket on his arm, and a crape round his hat, followed by* OLD SAM SCULLER, L.

Joe. (c.) And so we are to pull the gentleman down to the wharf, eh?

> Where the timber from the Swedish coast is floating,
> There the gentlemen would go a boating.

Scu. (L. C.) Ay, and we must make haste, too ; he said he would be ready in a few minutes, so come along.

Joe. No, I can't go out without seeing Mary; there's no persuading her out of her melancholy—

> All day she sits in tears, as sure as my name's Tiller,
> Like a crying cherry-bum, or else a weeping willer.

I'll be bound, now, she's gone down to the church-yard to sit by the side of old Dame Hallyard's grave ; she's almost always there, and as for a smile on her face—

> They're as scarce to be met with as oysters in June weather,
> And as difficult as strawberries in winter time to gether.

Scu. Ah, the old dame was a mother to her ; and how she used to watch the poor old woman as she faded day by day ! why, you might see her sink inch by inch into the grave.

Joe. [*Melancholy.*] Yes; and Mary got as pale as a winding-sheet: bless her, I *must* see her for a moment, then I'll go to work; work's my comfort. I don't know how it is, but I feel a sort of a something hanging over me —it's very foolish, I know, but—

> When the blue devils is wexing your brain,
> You may drive them away, but they come back again.

Scu. Well, then, run down to the church-yard and look for her ; I'll go to the Hard and prepare the boat.

Joe. Agreed. [*Going in,* R., *and looking off.*] Ha, here she comes ! look at her dear eyes, they're quite red ; yet she endeavours to hide them from me as if my own symphonies didn't inform me.

Enter MARY, R. S. E., *very pale, in a plain neat half-mourning dress.*

Mary. [*Advancing with a melancholy smile, and giving her hand to Joe.*] Did you want me, Joseph ?

Joe. (L.) I was just waiting to say a word to you before I went down to the Hard : you are still fretting ; you shouldn't take on so, Mary, it's breaking my heart.

Mary. (R.) I won't then, Joe, for you're very kind to me ; I will endeavour to be cheerful, it is my duty to be so ; but I've had a dream, and I've been down to mother's grave, and I couldn't look upon the blue flowers I've planted there without crying a little—they seemed so like her own dear, bright old eyes ! Besides, there's a strange flower grown up among them—I didn't put it there, it came up of itself, like a message from the dead ! It's a—yes, Joe, it's a Forget me Not ! [*Sobbing.*] a Forget me Not !

Joe. [*With emotion.*] Well, well, we never can forget her.

Mary. Oh, never! I hope it will not die; pretty bud, to come of itself! I'll water it every day. Do you know, as I looked at it, I heard her dead voice say the words as sure as I stand here, so you must forgive me for being a little melancholy.

Joe. Yes, Mary, I'm rather low myself to-day; I had a dream—I thought my boat was run down, and I had a narrow escape of my life.

Mary. [*Anxiously.*] Heaven forbid! you are my last friend.

Joe. I was a fool to let it annoy me—

> Because it is a maxim, you see, my dearest Mary,
> That if we dream of one thing, it's sure to come con-tra-ry.

Scu. [*Coming forward,* c.] There's one thing I'm dreaming of that won't come contrary: if we don't go down to the boat, the gentleman will hire somebody else to row him down to the wharfs, and it's a guinea job.

[*Crosses to* R.

Joe. Right;

> And if we lose a guinea,
> I know who'll be a ninny.

I don't know when I shall be home, Mary, but Sculler will come with me. Come, cheer up a bit; go out and buy a few trinkums; call on Mrs. Strop, the barber's wife; she'll talk you into spirits. God bless you!

> Come along, my old chap, and let us diskiver,
> If the customer's ready to go down the river.

[*Going, but returns.*] Good by, Mary! good by!

[*Exit with Sculler,* R. S. E.

Mary. (c.) I have called on Mrs. Strop already, and I have seen a newspaper: the ship of my poor Harry has come home; but, ah! where is he? [*With great agony.*] Stay—stay, Mary! you mustn't think in this way now; yet there can be no crime in loving the dead. I loved Harry living, and I can't do wrong in loving his memory. I passed by the Hard, and I saw the wherry. Joe hasn't taken out his name, for I could see it through the bit of crape he has nailed over it. I looked and looked till I couldn't see boat or river; my head swam, and my heart beat. I'm a silly—silly girl! I ought to have died with his mother; but I feel I'm burning away. Ha! ha! I'm strong, but it won't last for ever; no—no! [*Abigail Holdforth heard singing without,* R.] Oh, here comes this silly girl to annoy me; I have no spirits for her prattle.

Enter ABIGAIL HOLDFORTH, *dressed in the height of vulgar fashion,* R.

Abi. (c.) [*Speaking rapidly.*] Just comed up to Battersea for a breath of hair; Lunnun is so smoky! We who gets our livelihood in the fashionable quarters, to be sure, is better off than them as vegetates in the purloins of the Mansion House; but to me, a native of the delightful city of Bullock-Smithy, it's all very condense and mistificatory. So I took advantage of having to measure Mrs. Fubsey, the great malster's wife, (who lives within a short distance) for a new Parisian corset, to rustificate for a day, or, rather, half a day; for I've got to take home Miss Jemina Jumper's, the dancing-master's daughter's, new yeller silk frock, and there a'n't a stitch done; but I would come to see you, for, you know, you first recommended me, and though my own talons have exasperated me into a first-rate Magazin des Modes, I never forgets that to your good nature I'm indebted from the first. But you don't look well: as Mrs. Cackle, the poulterer's wife, says, there's a melancholie conglomerification about you. [*A pause.*] What's the matter?

Mary. (L. c.) I am not well. [*Aside.*] She'll kill me with talk!

Abi. [*Twirling round, and showing off.*] Do you like this dress?—Pretty taste, isn't it?—You can't think how the fellers did stare at me! one sailor-gentleman, in particular: it struck me I'd seen his face afore;—at first I thought it was your Harry, but——

Mary. [*Starting at the name.*] Oh, do not—do not!—This is cruel!

Abi. I beg your pardon—I didn't think——But I must go to Mrs. Fubsey's: la! she is such a perdigious size round! Oh, now I think of it, there was somebody with the sailor-gentleman very like Watchful Waxend; but I was on the coach, and it couldn't be he. [*Going.*] Well, good morning. [*Returning.*] I must go, or Miss Jumper won't have the yeller frock, and the Magazin des Modes will lose its charackter for punctualarity. [*Going.*] Good morning, my dear! [*Returning.*] Remember me to all; good by!—Comment vous portez vous to you!—Mrs. Fubsey will be in such a way!—Bye! bye!

[*Courtesying, and talking herself off,* R.

Mary. The sailor-gentleman she saw!—That's like my dream. In my sleep I thought Harry had come back; there

he was with his manly face tanned by the sun, but looking
better than ever ; and his mother was crying with joy ; and
he was dressed like an officer, and opened his arms for me ;
and I tried and tried, but I couldn't move near him ; ye⁺
I saw him, and I heard him speak my name, and I fel!
sure that he loved me ;—and this was dreaming ! Oh ! 1
wish the sleep had lasted ! yes—how I wish I could have
died in that dream !—But I awoke, and I—[*Kneeling,
overcome with emotion.*] Oh, my heart !—Harry ! Harry !
[*Exit in an agony of tears,* L.

SCENE III.—*The Banks of the Thames, and the opposite shore in the distance—the house of Dame Hallyard,
with the shutters closed,* R. F.—*another house,* L. F.

Enter WATCHFUL WAXEND *from behind the house,* R.,
in the dress of a sailor, and smoking his pipe.

Wax. [*Surveying Dame Hallyard's house.*] Well, this
is all very odd !—I've been " round the house, and round
the house,'' as the riddle says; but every window is as
close as a clicker's seam, and Harry is waiting for me ̇all
this while in the road : he wouldn't come for fear of fright-
ening the old dame and Mary.—He needn't have been
afeard ; they've gone out for some frolic on the water.   I
hav'n't seen a soul I know.—Well, I'll go down to the
Crown and Crozier ; old Wall-it will remember me, for I
owes him two-and-ninepence.   But, first, to find Harry,
and then——

Enter HARRY HALLYARD, *hurriedly,* R.

Harry. Avast, lad !—Why didn't you come ?—You don't
know how my heart has been keeping reckoning of all the
time you've stayed.   Have you seen 'em ? may I go in ?—
[*Looking at the house,* R. F.] Belay, there ! I'm taken
right aback !—What's the meaning of all these dead-lights
being hung out ?—Have they shifted their anchorage ?—
Have they fallen foul of any misfortune ?—Where's my
Poll ? where—where's the old mother ?—Speak ! say out
what intelligence you've got, or I shall founder with the
trembles !

Wax. (L. C.) The house is shut up !

Harry. (C.) I see—I see !

Wax. I've been round it, and can't find a hole to peep
in at.

Harry. Well—well !

Wax. So I conclude——

Harry. What—what?

Wax. That Joe's giving 'em a bit of a nautical discursion on the river.

Harry. Right, lad! that's it!—My heart was up in my throat!—There's no harm happened to the old craft, that the young one has been obliged to sail from her moorings? No! no!—Joe would take care of that—I know him.— Joe's a true heart!—It's hard, though, within sight of port, to be blown out to sea again in this fashion. What's to be done?

Wax. I know what I shall do: I shall bear down to the Crown and Crozier, and old Sculler's.

Harry. Good—they'll spin you a yarn. Crowd all sail! while I tack about these latitudes.—I can't leave the old spot. [*Hurrying him off.*] Come, lad, bear a hand, and be back in the turning of a handspike!

Wax. [*Going,* L.] I'll be back before you can wax a thread. [*Returning.*] You stay here, my boy: I'll hoist a signal that shall put a sparable in your heel, and I'll stick to you like wax!

Harry. [*Impatiently.*] Aye! aye! [*Exit Waxend,* L.] No, I can't leave the old house, though there is nobody to welcome me. I thought I should have been scrunched up with kissings and huggings, and hard shakings before now; and here, after five years of danger, no one knows me: the old house shuts its doors against me, and there's no Polly— no mother—no friend! Well, well! they didn't expect me. My eyes! how glad they will be to see me when they do come!—What a fool I am! [*Crossing to the house,* L.] I don't know who lives here? But they'll give me some chart to steer by. I'll knock and ax a question or two. [*Knocking, and coming forward,* R. C.] Yes, there's the old garden, and the little dock where I used to launch all the small craft I cut out of the bits of wood I got from Charley Chips, the carpenter! Ah! my pretty Polly was a young one then!—Law! how she used to laugh to see 'em sail away lop-sided down the river!—Bless her!

Enter MARY *from the house,* L. F.

Mary. Was it you knocked at our——

Harry. [*Starting suddenly.*] Ha! that voice! [*Turning, and seeing her.*] Mary! [*Advancing a step or two— she recedes, gazing at him.*] Mary! my own Polly!— Don't you know me?—Harry, my girl—Harry!

Mary. [*As if awaking from a dream.*] Alive! [*Scream-ing with joy.*] Harry! my Harry!

[*She springs into his arms, and instantly faints.*

Harry. Gently, my little tender one! But I hardly know myself whether *my* senses won't desert the flag.— Lord love her pretty pale face!—Joy's colours I see are white. [*Kissing her.*] Polly, lass, cheerly—cheerly!— Come, don't shut the port of your pretty peepers to give your sailor his welcome, like the old mother's house there. Mary—my precious Mary! Ha! her recollection's heav-ing to; there—there!

Mary. [*Partially reviving, and looking vacantly around, as if striving to recollect.*] I thought that——

Harry. Mary!

Mary. 'Tis he!—'Tis so, then; my dear Harry, you are alive and—[*Rushing into his arms, but recollecting herself, and screaming.*] No! [*Shuddering back.*] No! Don't come near me—don't touch me, Harry!—don't touch me, I say!—It is past!—Oh, cruel deceit!—Don't touch me! I dare not—I——Oh! my brain is bursting!

Harry. [*Seiziug her arm.*] What does this mean?

Mary. Oh, for mercy's sake! unhand me! you must not come near me! I am——I cannot speak the word! Let go—let go! [*Struggling wildly.*] I shall go mad! [*Break-ing from him.*] There—there! Oh, pity me! when you know all, pity me!

[*Rushes distractedly into the house,* L. F.

Harry. [*Thunderstruck.*] When I know all! What all? Is this my fond Mary that——Oh, I'm dreaming! [*Rubbing his eyes.*] Not come near her!

Enter OLD SAM SCULLER, *hastily and agitated,* R.—*he crosses as if going to the house,* L. F.

Harry. [*Catching his arm.*] Avast heaving, old man! A word or two with you.

Scu. Don't stay me: I'm on business of life and death!

Harry. Your answer is life or death to me. Don't you know me, old boy? Why, you ar'n't altered a bit.

Scu. [*In astonishment.*] Why, no!—What! can it be Harry Hallyard?

Harry. It is.

Scu. (L. C.) We thought you dead.

Harry. (C.) [*Eagerly.*] Why's the old house shut up? Where's my mother?—Why does Mary fly from me?— Tell me quick, old man: my brain's on fire!

Scu. [*Half aside.*] Oh, unhappy business! when he knows all——

Harry. When I know all!—What is there for me to know? Out with the worst. My mother——

Scu. Lies in yonder churchyard.

Harry. [*Staggering.*] Dead!—Poor old mother! and I not here to close her eyes! [*A pause.*] Mary—

Scu. Mary is—I—I can't tell you.

Harry. Oh, do, old man: if you have any mercy—if you have any recollection of your green days, when your heart loved, and—speak! speak!

Scu. It must be told. Mary is—Mary is married!

Harry. [*Paralised.*] God! married?—Mary, that I've loved so truly, married! Oh! [*Laughing hysterically.*] Ha! ha! ha!—It's a lie! [*Wildly.*] You may as well trifle with a hungry shark!—Come, tell the truth!—Yet she wouldn't come near me. I'm surely going mad!— Who's her—her——you know what I mean.

Scu. Her husband. Joe—your partner Joe.

Harry. [*Nearly falling.*] Oh, is—is this——

[*He tries in vain to speak, at length bursts into a passion of tears, and throws himself upon the shoulders of Sculler.*

Scu. [*Supporting him.*] My poor noble Harry! I won't attempt to comfort you—words would be in vain; but they were not to blame—I am their witness.

Harry. [*With sarcastic energy.*] Not to blame?—Oh, no! falsehood isn't a fault, treachery isn't a crime. I have been five years away, but I have never for a moment forgotten her; I have worn this lock of hair upon my heart day and night, in the battle, the storm, and the calm, ever since, and her name, my old mother's, and his, have been oftener on my lips than my prayers, and dearer to me than the life I ventured. Well, I come back; I—I find her false—the friend I loved a villain—and my poor mother cold and dead! And although their treachery—no! oh, no! —they are not to blame! I—I—Curse it! I wish the tears didn't come up in this way—they are fire! Here, here, take my money—take my watch—take all! [*Putting them into the hands of Sculler.*] I earned all for their sake, and now I have lost them. [*Going,* R.

Scu. [*Detaining him.*] Stay, you shall see Joe; I have just come from him, poor fellow! he was well an hour ago —I am going to tell Mary —they are bringing him here.

Harry. [*Anxiously.*] Why, what's the matter?

E

Scu. In helping to unload a barge, the crane-chain snapped, it fell on him, and he is all but dead.

Harry. Um—hark ye : break it to her gently—she'll suffer much—she'll be able to guess what my heart feels ; tell her gently, and quickly, too. [*Aside.*] She must not founder on the banks of poverty! Oh, my brain! [*To Sculler.*] I'll wait for you. Now be gentle, old man ; she's but a tender thing. Come, come. [*Exit into the house,* L. F.

SCENE IV.—*An Apartment, with a large opening,* c. f., *covered by a checkered curtain, which, when withdrawn, discovers a neatly furnished room, with a glass door,* c., *standing open, discovering the garden, the river, and opening shore beyond.*

Enter MARY, *in excessive agitation,* c. f., *dragging a chair after her, and holding an old newspaper in her hand— her manner is wild and hurried in the extreme—she seats herself,* c.

Mary. [*With trembling eagerness.*] I can't see, my eyes flash fire—I wish that I could cry! I did see it here—no, no! [*Searching the paper.*] Ha! there, dead! dead! and yet I have seen him—I have heard him call me his Mary, and I have lived to know myself another's! Oh ! if I could but sink into his mother's grave, and he never know—but he will know, and he will loathe me—he will curse me! Oh, do not—do not, Harry, curse me! no, no! the old woman begged it with tears in her dying eyes—he wou't believe me—he laughs! Oh, God! I—would I could die at your feet, Harry, that you might see my heart! I was true ; I—oh, don't spurn—I——

Enter OLD SAM SCULLER, c. f.—*she falls insensibly from the chair.*

Scu. [*Coming forward,* c.] Poor broken-hearted girl ! she breathes !

    [*He goes up, pulls back the curtain, discovering the room, and Harry Hallyard anxiously peeping in at the glass-door, and supporting himself by the door-post.*

Scu. [*Beckoning him.*] Look here, Harry, the poor thing's fainted !

Enter HARRY—*he advances and gazes for a moment on her—Sculler is going to raise her.*

Harry. [*Preventing him.*] No, no, let her lie still ; I

hear a noise of voices—they are bringing him—lead 'em round another way—she must be told first.

Scu. Right!   *[Exit cautiously, on tip-toe,* c. f.

Harry. [Gazing sorrowfully on her.] There she lies in her pale beauty, like a moon-beam on the stilled waters of the ocean! What a pity she should be as cold as the one and as fickle as the other! All my world is on that little spot of earth! Oh! if she could conceive how I love her! even *her* changing heart would weep for me; but she can't —no, no! she knows nothing of the lovely hopes and the sweet longings of a real love—even now false to me—another's! My soul is pouring out of my eyes in adoration! I will raise her off the ground, 'tis a course bed for so tender a flower. *[Raising her.]* I cannot resist the impulse! she will not know that I have stolen that which is now another's—'twill be the last—*[Kissing her.]*—the last, the last, and for ever!

Re-enter Old Sam Sculler, c. f.

Scu. I don't see them yet; has she recovered?

Harry. [Raising her.] I think her recollection's heaving to. Here, take her, old man, take her.

    [Sculler receives her in his arms—Harry, overpowered with emotion, leans on the chair, and weeps.

Mary. [Recovering.] It is true! he is dead, and—mother, don't cry so! I—oh, my brain! *[Looking round wildly, and seeing Harry.]* Oh, I remember now!

    [She rushes to the paper, holds it up to Harry, pointing in agony to the place, and throws herself on her knees.

Scu. 'Tis the paper with the account of your death.

Harry. What of that? had she loved, she would have hoped it was false, she would have gone down to—to her grave, as——   *[Overpowered with emotion.*

Mary. [Still kneeling to him.] Would to heaven I had, Harry! How did I prove my love? though 'tis sin in me to speak of it now. Two, three, four years elapsed, and no letters from you, but I never doubted—I tried to prove my love for you by performing all the duties of a daughter to your mother; still time went on; at last the news came that you were killed—we saw it in the newspaper—Joe got the list from the Admiralty—there we saw it again—I won't say how my heart was bleeding as I watched your poor old mother dying with the news—she and I wept together, and prayed for the peace; I saw she was sinking, too; she

trembled to leave me : for your sake she pointed to Joe as
a protector—for your sake she begged, and, to let her die
in peace, for your sake, Harry, I consented—I became a
wife, but I still loved, I still wept in secret, though duty
made me silent.   Go ! it is a broken heart now, and my
hand is another's, but it is yours till the grave—till—oh,
pity ! oh, pity, and forgive !

  [*She sinks exhausted, and is supported by Sculler.*

  Harry. I do ! I do ! but can't believe that you—no—I
have stayed to tell you that there is money—I have earned
it for your sake, and if you wish to—not quite to kill me,
you will use it.

  Mary. No, oh, no !
  Harry. You will, Mary !
  Mary. Oh, spare me !
  Harry. You will obey me, if you wish me to forget—
forget ! oh, that's as impossible as that I should ever cease
to love.   But you may have need of it ; the shoals of ad-
versity arn't always to be avoided ; even now you are
among the breakers.   There it is. [*Putting it on the
table.*] And now—the old man there will explain ; I forgive you, but I don't wish to curse him.   God bless you !

  [*Going.*

  Mary. [*On her knees, clinging to him.*] Oh, pity !
  Harry. I do ! I do ! and do you pity me.

  [*He breaks from her, and rushing up,* c., *pulls the
    curtain aside, and is met by Watermen, &c., bear-
    ing in Joe, wounded—Mary shrieks, and runs to
    him—Harry comes down,* R.

  Mary. [*Attending.*] He is my husband !
  Harry. [*Covering his eyes with his hands, and standing
immovable.*] Right ! right !
  Joe. [*Faintly.*] Bless you, Mary !—I hoped to see you
again, for—I—I had heard of Harry's return, and I wished
to say something before I died, to prove that you were in-
nocent of falsehood to him.
  Mary. Don't speak—you are bleeding.
  Joe. I am ; but I must speak.   Harry thinks I am a
villain, but do explain.   I'm faint !
  Mary. I have told him—I—
  Joe. And is he convinced ?
  Harry. Joe, I grieve to see you thus ; but unless my
mother's voice from the grave assured me of——
  Joe. Hold !   Here—here—here's your mother's will,
where she leaves the sticks in the cottage, and the wherry,

and all to me, to marry Mary. You'll see how she urges it for your sake. Read, Harry, read!—That is her voice from the grave!

Harry. [*Looking at the will.*] Poor old mother!

[*Kisses it, and weeps.*

Joe. Do you forgive her—forgive Mary?

Harry. [*Dropping on his knee by his side.*] I do.

Mary. And Joe?

Harry. Yes, yes!

Joe. Then I'm happy.—I'm dying!—Harry! Mary!

[*He pulls their hands together, joins them in front of himself, and dies across them.*

Harry. He is dead!—Mary!

Mary. Harry! Harry!

[*They rush into each other's arms, recollect themselves, and kneel in prayer by the side of Joe—the others take off their hats, and surround him, and the curtain slowly descends.*

DISPOSITION OF THE CHARACTERS AT THE FALL OF THE CURTAIN.

		Watermen.		*Watermen.*	
		JOE.			
Females.	HARRY.		MARY.		SCULLER.
R.]					[L.

THE END.